LOVING QUINN

ALICIA MONTGOMERY

Loving Quinn

Book 2 of the Lone Wolf Defenders

By

Alicia Montgomery

ALSO BY ALICIA MONTGOMERY

The True Mate Series

Fated Mates

Blood Moon

Romancing the Alpha

Witch's Mate

Taming the Beast

Tempted by the Wolf

The Lone Wolf Defenders Series

Killian's Secret

Loving Quinn

All for Connor

To my amazing readers. You rock.

1
———

*T*he well-worn manila envelope sat on his desk, its presence like an itch that Quinn couldn't scratch. Why he placed it there, where it was always in the corner of his eye, he didn't know. His name was scrawled in a familiar handwriting, but it had remained sealed since he found it weeks ago. Archie Leacham had left his adopted children many things when he died—his mansion in Portland, priceless treasures, and boatloads of cash. Yet, this was one thing Quinn was reluctant to inherit. When the old master thief had adopted him and his Lone Wolf siblings, he compiled all these files about their backgrounds, but never gave it to them until his death.

Quinn had never believed in looking back at the past. It was done, after all, and he refused to think of the before. Before Archie, before his sister and brothers. Because before was growing up with a single mother who could barely put food on the table. Before was hospitals and the stench of death. Before was the string of foster homes and harsh words and bruises and broken noses.

A low growl escaped from his throat. *Calm down, buddy.* Wolf was not always easy to manage, but Archie had taught

Quinn to control it. For a human, his adoptive father knew a lot about shifters, having been married to a Lycan himself. Quinn knew if it wasn't for Archie, the animal would have broken apart. Still, Wolf did not like to be reminded of the past.

He grabbed the envelope, opened the bottom drawer of his desk, and shoved it inside, right on top of the spare cables and wires he always kept there just in case. Leaning back in his chair, he looked at the multiple screens he had set up on his desk, checking the programs he was running. As Lone Wolf Security's resident computer guy and hacker, he was responsible for all things tech for their operations.

Right now, he was running some background checks, tapping into various government databases, and looking at images from a string of satellites he had hacked into. While he and his brothers had turned legit, he wasn't breaking about a thousand international laws just for profit. No, he was doing this for good. A few months ago, when the Lycans had their final confrontation with their enemies, the evil mages had left behind an army of shifter slaves. These Lycans were Lone Wolves, like him and his siblings, who had been ripped apart from their clans on purpose. Aside from running security ops for their parent company, Creed Security, Quinn, Killian, and Connor made it their mission to reunite the Lone Wolves with their families.

The irony of his work was not lost on him. He used his skills to help those Lone Wolves find out about their past, yet his was sitting in the bottom of his desk drawer, waiting for him. Killian and Meredith had apparently opened theirs. Meredith wasn't interested in knowing her former clan, and Killian's were all gone. And Connor? Well, he didn't know what Connor was up to these days. His brother had always been secretive about his past and, even now, refused to say if he had opened his envelope.

Despite the resources he had at his fingertips, reuniting the Lost Wolves with their families was still taking time. There were about thirty of them, plus the additional Lycans they had rescued from their last op. Plus, he also had some legit security work he was supposed to do for his boss, Sebastian Creed. But Quinn wasn't worried. He never missed a deadline and he never let anyone down. Just because he and his brothers went legit, didn't mean he was going to start slacking off. He had a few hours of nothing to do and, glancing at the clock, he realized it was nearly noon. *Awesome.* That meant only one thing ...

Quinn got up from the chair and glanced at his reflection in the window. He was dressed casually, as usual, in a black tight-fitting shirt and jeans. His longish blond hair was in need of a trim, but running his hands quickly through the locks put them in some semblance of order. There was a couple days of scruff on his jaw, but he knew that always drove the ladies wild.

"Hey, Evie." Quinn greeted Lone Wolf Security's part time administrative assistant. Evie King was seated at the reception desk, typing up the latest report on their last mission. "It's almost noon, aren't you going to lunch?"

"Hmmm?" She looked up at him, then at the clock. "Oh, yeah. I guess I'll order in a sandwich from the deli or something. You want me to get you one, too?"

He frowned. "Aren't you going out? Weather's finally warming up. And surely Selena would rather be out in the park than stuck in here."

"Oh, Selena's not coming today," Evie replied and turned back to the computer screen.

Quinn waited for a heartbeat or two, but Evie did not elaborate. Selena always stopped for lunch by the Lone Wolf office on the days Evie came in. She mentioned she didn't work too far away. Why wasn't she coming today?

A stab of disappointment went through Quinn, and he told

himself it was only because he was looking forward to his usual verbal sparring with his archenemy. Selena ... whatever her last name was. Every time she would stop by to pick up Evie for lunch, Quinn made sure he was there to prod and provoke the curvy little witch. He couldn't help it; it was too fun to watch her blue-gray eyes blaze in anger whenever he was around, and so he did it every chance he got. Of course, she also gave as good as she got and shot back with her own insults. He looked forward to her visits, thinking up new ways to annoy her each time.

"Is she sick?" Quinn finally asked.

"Who?"

"Selena. Is she sick?"

"No, she just came home really late last night. I think she had a date," Evie said casually. "Anyway, she just texted me that she's staying at the library for lunch since she slept in."

A small pit formed in Quinn's stomach. Selena had a date, and she didn't come home until this morning. Wolf was growling, setting his teeth on edge. Why Wolf acted that way, he didn't know. He really needed to get a hold of his animal. Damn thing was ruling his life these days. "Must have been a good date," he managed to say out loud. "What's his name?"

Before she could answer, the door slammed open and Evie nearly jumped out of her chair. Connor's large frame filled the door, his expression dour. So, normal for him. The scar over the right side of his face deepened as he looked over at Evie, then quickly glanced away.

"Well, good morning, sunshine," Quinn greeted.

Connor grunted in reply. "I'm only here because Killian's on his honeymoon. Again. How many honeymoons does one man need?"

Quinn laughed. "That first one was a baby moon," he pointed out. "This is the real, after the wedding honeymoon."

"Whatever. Don't bother me unless you need to." He disappeared down the hallway, and the sound of his heavy footsteps were followed by the slamming of the door.

"Hey," Quinn said, calling Evie's attention. Her gaze was stuck toward the hallway, and Quinn rolled his eyes. Connor and Evie had been playing eye ping-pong for months now, but neither had spoken more than two words when they were in the same room. Of course, that probably had to do with the fact that when they first met, she hit him with her purse. But that was ages ago. The tension between the two of them had been growing, and Quinn wished they'd put themselves (and everyone else) out of their misery and just fuck already. It would probably help get that stick out of his brother's ass.

"So, who is he?"

"Who?" Evie asked, taken out of her trance.

"Selena's date."

"She didn't say."

God, this is like pulling teeth, Quinn moaned to himself. Even Wolf was getting annoyed, letting out a huff and scratching at him. He just wanted to know who this guy was so he could run a background check and make sure he wasn't some serial killer. He could also break into the guy's social networks and maybe his email just to be doubly safe. It wouldn't hurt. But how could he do it if he didn't know who she was with? He'd have to take matters into his own hands.

"So, sandwich from the deli?" Evie asked.

"Nah," he said, shaking his head. "I think I'll go outside. Enjoy the spring sunshine." He grabbed his phone from his pocket and pulled up his browser. *So, the little witch worked at the library.* With some Google-fu, he could probably figure out which library Selena worked at. After all, if she had an hour lunch and she had time to stop by Lone Wolf during her break, she probably didn't work too far.

$\mathcal{S}$ elena Merlin yawned for the umpteenth time that morning, not even bothering to stifle the sound coming from her mouth. She adjusted her glasses and tried to focus on the screen in front of her. Normally, the Dewey Decimal System came naturally to her, but today, it just wasn't making sense.

She supposed she deserved it, staying out all night like that, but how could she possibly resist the all-night Star Wars Marathon at the Odeon theater? Sure, she stumbled home at three a.m., but it was worth it. Besides, it wasn't like working at the Lower Manhattan library was exciting. It was a boring, nine-to-five job, but at least she got to work in New York City.

Growing up in Philadelphia, all she wanted to do was escape her family. She loved her life there, but she couldn't stand another minute of living with her stepmother and stepsisters. Her father Leonard had married another witch from the coven two years after her mother's death. Jane wasn't cruel to her, but she definitely favored her own daughters over Selena. Alexis and Katrina, on the other hand, tormented her every chance they got. After she graduated from college, she found a job at the New York Public Library and only went back home for visits, mostly so she could stop by her mother's grave.

Unable to stay awake, she decided putting books back in the stacks might help. She stood up and smoothed down her pencil skirt and blouse, glad to finally be able to wear her spring clothes. She hated winter, mostly because bulky sweaters and coats did nothing for her figure. Being top-heavy, she looked frumpy when she added layers over her body. Now, she could get back to wearing her normal office clothes even outside and show off her curvy hourglass figure. Not that anyone looked at her. There were so many gorgeous girls in New York, all tall, stick thin, and beautiful. Who would notice a petite, curvy girl with unremarkable features (not to mention curly red hair that turned into a rat's nest if she didn't spend a shit ton of money on products) when there was always a buffet of models around? Still, it shouldn't bother her. She should be used to being invisible by now.

Selena grabbed the rolling cart and pushed it down the aisle, stopping to place the books on their proper shelves as she moved along the rows. She emptied the cart until there was one book left. Ah, a biography of Winston Churchill. Of course, this one was all the way in the back. Just her luck, it was also on a high shelf.

She faced her enemy—the top shelf. Standing on her tiptoes, Selena held the thick book in her fingertips and then lifted it high, pushing it into the small space between the biographies of Chopin and Cicero.

The sound of someone clearing his throat surprised her, and the book slipped from her fingers, landing with a loud thud on the floor.

"Motherfucking shit. Who the fuck—" She stopped short when her eyes landed on the person at the end of the aisle. An involuntary gasp left her lips and warmth crept up her neck.

Quinn stood there, casually leaning against the shelf, his muscled arms crossed over his chest. His black shirt stretched deliciously across his broad shoulders, and the smile he had on his handsome face sent her nerve endings stirring. God, he looked yummy today, and the temperature spiked a few degrees.

"You kiss your mother with that mouth, Butterfingers?"

Selena let out a puff of breath, blowing a stray strand of auburn curls away from her face. Right. There was no doubt Quinn was handsome as sin and sexy as hell, but the moment he opened his mouth, the only thing Selena wanted to do was smack him upside the head. For some reason, ever since they met, the Lycan had zeroed in on her and teased her mercilessly. Not that she couldn't hold her own, but part of her was getting tired of always being on guard around him.

"I wouldn't have dropped it if you didn't creep around here like some ... creeper." She bent down and grabbed the book, but, suddenly, Quinn was right there next to her. He reached for the book, snatching it away.

"Here, let me get that," he said in an annoyed voice.

"I can do it myself," she huffed.

"Is that so, short stack?" Quinn looked at the book. "Is that why Mr. Churchill ended up on the ground?" He tsked and looked at the book sadly. "Not very dignified, right Winston? Why didn't you get a ladder or something?"

"I was trying to save some time; this was the last book. What are you—" She held her breath when he stepped forward. She staggered back, and Quinn's large body trapped her against the shelf behind her. The familiar scent of his aftershave wafted into her nose—freshly cut grass and sawdust. Her knees nearly buckled underneath her, but she steadied herself. He was so close she could feel the warmth of his body.

"See?" Quinn said, nodding up at the shelf. "You should try being taller, that will really save you time."

Selena looked up at him, and he stared right back. The Nordic blue of his eyes seemed to bore right into her, and she swallowed a gulp. The last time they had been this close together, they were stuck inside a supply closet a few weeks ago. Those few minutes in close quarters seemed like hours, and she started to panic and hyperventilate. As she heaved and gasped, she felt a warm hand stroke her back soothingly, the touch sending tingles across her skin. She had been unnerved at the unfamiliar sensation, not to mention, something hard poking at her butt that she was pretty sure wasn't a banana in his pocket. Her reaction was to immediately lash out at Quinn once they were out, something she still regretted.

"I'll try it next time," she retorted and then pushed him gently. Jeez, did he work out like, six times a day? His chest was solid, and the muscles underneath were like rock under her palms. "What are you doing here anyway?" she asked.

Quinn stepped back and then flashed her another smile. "I just realized I don't have a library card," he explained. "I thought it was time I got one."

She let out a laugh. "Aren't real books too analog for you? I thought you spend all your time in front of a computer?"

"Hey, that hurts," he replied, putting his hand over his heart. "Of course I read books. So, would you happen to know any librarians who can help me out?" He flashed her a lopsided smile.

"Fine," she said wryly. "Follow me."

She led him back to her desk and motioned for him to stand in front of the black paneling. "All right, I'll go ahead and put in the Lone Wolf Security office as your address, but tell me your full name."

"You know what it is," he answered.

"Yes, I know your first name, but what's your last name?"

"I don't have one," he said. "I'm a Lone Wolf, remember? No clan, no last name."

"Well, I have to put something in," she said in an exasperated voice.

"Put in whatever you want, babe," he replied. "Whatever you think works, as long as I can get my card."

Selena rolled her eyes and sighed, then typed in the first thing that popped into her mind. "All right then," she said as she reached toward the printer and took out the card. "Here you go." She handed it to him with a sweet smile.

Quinn took the card, and when his eyes scanned the front, he let out a chuckle. Selena frowned, not expecting his reaction. At the very least, she thought he would have had some snappy comeback.

"Quinn McFuckface?" He chuckled. "I walked into that one." He tucked the card into his back pocket.

"I just hope your poor future wife won't mind being called 'Mrs. McFuckface,'" she retorted.

"No chance of that, seeing as I'm never getting married."

Selena gave him a tight smile. She didn't know why, but that admission sent a pang of disappointment through her. "Right," she said as she stood up. "Now, if you're done, I have to be getting back to work." She motioned to the cart full of books next to her desk.

"Did you get any lunch yet?" he asked. "It must be your lunch break or something."

"I came in a little late today," she explained. "Slept in. So, I'm trying to make up for it."

"Right, your hot date."

"My what?" she said with a laugh.

"Evie said—I mean, she seemed disappointed when you couldn't come for lunch," Quinn replied. "She told me you were out on a date and didn't come back until this morning. So, tell me, who's the guy?"

"Harrison Ford," she said quickly.

"Oh, is he—what?" He frowned. "Are you shitting me?"

"I was at the Star Wars marathon at the Odeon," Selena explained. "They started late, but I couldn't leave. They had actual film prints from the original trilogy, and I had to sit through those awful prequels just to see them."

"I didn't know you were a nerd," Quinn moaned.

"Damn right," she answered. "Anyway, I guess I'll see you around." Selena turned to leave, but a hand on her arm stopped her. "What?" she asked, ignoring the tingles his touch sent over her skin.

"So, you haven't eaten?"

"I told you, I don't have time. I'll grab a candy bar from the vending machine or something." She frowned at his hand, which remained firmly around her arm.

"C'mon, you can't survive on just a candy bar the whole day. I saw a hotdog cart on the corner; I'm sure you can spare fifteen minutes for a quick bite." He flashed her another smile. "I'll even buy you one."

Selena hesitated for a moment. "Fine. But you don't need to buy me a hotdog. This isn't a date."

"I didn't say it was," he retorted. "I don't date unless the girl's planning to put out."

"Then we're in agreement because I'm not putting out for you," she shot back quickly.

"Yeah, whatever. Let's go. I'm starving."

*T*hey both got hot dogs and soda from the cart across the street, then made their way back to the steps outside the library. As promised, Selena paid for her meal, but also insisted paying for his. After a brief squabble, she handed the vendor a twenty and grabbed the food.

Why Selena said yes to Quinn, she wasn't sure. Still, it was a nice day with spring finally arriving. The weather was warming up, and she didn't even need to put on her light jacket to go outside.

"I didn't know you worked at a library," Quinn said after he finished his hot dog in two bites.

"I told you I worked near your office," she replied. "It's nice to see Evie during the day. She's usually out at night, working at the diner or doing an open mic, and I don't get to see her when I get home."

"How did you become friends?"

Selena laughed. "She came to the library to check her email. Poor thing was new in town, and she didn't have a computer or internet access so she could find out about casting calls. I knew New York was going to chew her up and spit her out if I didn't take her under my wing. We became friends, and then she moved in with me to help with the rent. Eventually, she also figured out my background and confessed that her mother's a Lycan." She shrugged.

"So she found your stash of eye of newt lying around? Or your broom?"

"Ha! It was actually the dried lavender I have around the apartment. My mother always had it for protection. Anyway, it works out—I get to save money and she doesn't have to bunk with six other girls in a fleabag hotel room in Hell's Kitchen."

"What about your coven? Aren't you witches supposed to

live together or something? Communal living and all that hippy dippy shit?"

"We don't have to live together, but most of us do," she said.

"So, like, what can you do? Do you control wind or thunder or something cool?" he asked.

"No," she retorted. "Magic doesn't work like that. For the most part, witches and warlocks have the ability to activate spells and potions. While anyone can mix ingredients or say a few magical words, only a witch can infuse magic into them. What you're talking about is called 'blessed magic,' which are active powers that only very few witches have." Indeed, Selena herself only knew of two people who had active powers—Quinn's brother-in-law Daric and her distant relative Lara Chatraine. "And like I told you when we first met, I'm an almost witch."

"I still don't know what it means." He took a swig of his soda. "So, what the heck is an almost witch?"

"Well, my father is a warlock, and my mother was a witch. She was actually from the New York coven and distantly related to Charlotte Fontaine, who was kind of a big deal in our history. Anyway," Selena continued, "they both had magic, and, usually, witches come into power right around puberty."

"So?" Quinn looked at her quizzically.

"Well, I'm still waiting for my power to come in. I'm told it will. Eventually."

"Oh, so you're just a human now."

Selena flinched visibly, and it probably would have hurt less if Quinn had physically struck her. Perhaps she'd been in denial all these years, but it helped ease the pain. She was born from two powerful bloodlines, yet here she was, showing no magical talent whatsoever. Selena the Dud. That was the cruel nickname her stepsisters, who were real witches, gave her. It followed her around most of her teen life, and she could remember nights when she cried herself to sleep, wishing—no, begging—to feel even a drop of magic within her.

Balling her hands into fists, she stood up. "I should go." Without a backward glance, she walked away, the heels of her stilettos clicking on the pavement in military fashion.

"Hey!" Quinn called, but she ignored him. "Selena, stop!" He quickly caught up to her, and he grabbed her arm. "C'mon," he said, his voice softening. "Did I say something wrong?"

Selena felt her chin tremble, but she bit the inside of her cheek to keep the tears from spilling. "Let go of me, Quinn," she managed to say in a shaky voice.

"Hey, hey now," he soothed and attempted to place his hands on her shoulder. "What's wrong? Are you on your period or something? 'Cause I know girls can be kinda emotional and bitchy when they're on—"

"Shut up!" Selena yelled, wrenching away from him. Anger was bubbling in her now, and she just wanted to be alone. "I don't know what you have against me, Quinn," she began. "But I'm sick and tired of it! You ... you just stay the hell away from now on!"

3

"What the fuck did I do?" Quinn wondered aloud as he watched Selena storm back into the library. One moment they were having a nice lunch and he was teasing her, and then she just got all huffy and stomped away. "Women," he muttered as he slammed his trash into the bin.

A psychologist probably would have said Quinn hated women, with the way he went through them like tissues. But that was far from it. Quinn loved women. He loved all kinds of women. Maybe that was the problem. He wanted to please all of them, a little too much, and that was sometimes what got him in trouble.

But Selena was different. He wanted to see the fire in her eyes, wanted her to react to him needling her and dish it right back. Quinn enjoyed the challenge, but something he said today pushed her over the edge. He should just forget about her. Find some chick, go back to her place ... shit. He couldn't remember the last time he'd gotten his dick wet. Hmmm ... that girl he took to Nobu, maybe? She had been fun, but a little too clingy. Wanted him to stay the night. Yeah, right. Anyway, that was the last time he saw some action, other than his hand. He was just too busy. That was it. Too many cases, too much work. It wasn't because of the way Selena's tight little skirt hugged her ass or the glasses that made her look like every boy's sexy librarian wet dream. Nuh-uh. It especially wasn't her juicy little mouth or her butterscotch scent he found intoxicating and seemed to drive Wolf crazy whenever he had a sniff. Even now, the animal was whining in disappointment and growling at him for making Selena angry.

Yeah, he should just forget about Selena. It was fun while it lasted, but she was obviously too sensitive to take a joke.

Quinn walked back to the office, already planning to head out to Blood Moon that night. Maybe he could find some hot Lycan girl to hook up with. Wolf let out a growl, and he told the thing to take a chill pill. Damn animal. Why was it mad at him?

"Hey, what the hell is wrong with your friend?" Quinn asked Evie as he walked in. The brunette was already putting her coat on and shutting down her computer.

"Selena?" Evie asked with a frown. "What do you mean? What did you hear?"

"I went to take her to lunch and we were talking, then she goes mental on me," Quinn relayed.

"What?" Evie snapped her head up. "What do you mean you took her to lunch?"

"I went to the library," Quinn explained. "And then we ate hotdogs, and I asked her what an almost witch was, and she explained."

Evie narrowed her eyes. "And then what did you say?"

Quinn thought for a moment. "I pointed out she was human, and then she went insane."

"You said that?" Evie's voice pitched higher, and she walked around her desk to face him. "You idiot!" She grabbed her purse and slammed it on his shoulder.

"Oh! Jeez, now I know why Connor's still mad at you—that fucking hurt!"

"Quinn, you're such a jerk!" Evie raised her purse again, but he blocked it with his arms. "Don't you know how insulting that is?"

"Well, it's true, isn't it?" Quinn shrugged. "Witches are basically humans with powers, so if she doesn't have magic, then, duh, she's human."

"Ugh, you are impossible." Evie let out an exasperated sigh. "Look, my mother is a Lycan and my dad is human, which means I'm human too. In our world, that doesn't mean anything, and I don't mind being labeled a human, but it's different with witches. Their status is determined by the amount of power they have and Selena, who doesn't have any powers, is at the bottom rung in the coven. A fact that they never let her forget."

"Jesus fucking Christ." Quinn slapped his hand on his forehead. "I am a fucking jerk." He realized how much he had insulted Selena. *I basically rubbed it in her face that she was powerless.* And Wolf was now scratching at his middle angrily.

"Yeah, you and your big fat mouth." Evie sighed. "Just leave her alone, okay? And stop trying to provoke her. Why you pick on her, I don't know."

Shit. Leave her alone? Would that really be the solution? "Look, I need to tell her I'm sorry." *And I need her to forgive me*, he added silently. He had a feeling that ache in his chest wouldn't be going away until she did. Wolf certainly wasn't going to leave him in peace, either. "How can I make it up to her?"

Evie crossed her arms over her chest. "You promise not to hurt her anymore?"

"I promise."

"Or insult her or provoke her?"

"Yeah, yeah, I promise, okay?"

"All right. There is something ..."

---

*T*he next day, Quinn found himself at the entrance of the Lower Manhattan Library once again. *Get it together*, he told himself. She's just a woman, no big deal. But for some reason, his palms were sweaty and that annoyed the shit out of him.

The familiar scent of paper, leather, and wood hit his nose as he walked inside. It brought back memories of Archie's library in the Portland mansion and the hours Quinn spent there as a teen. Walking by Selena's desk, he saw it was empty, but there was a sign on the table that read: *Storytime at 4:30 p.m: Children's Section.*

After taking a quick glance at the map, he went to the second floor where he found Selena sitting on a chair in the middle of the carpeted area. A dozen children surrounded her, all looking up in rapt attention as she read from a storybook.

"And so the Big Bad Wolf said, 'Come out little piggy, or I'll huff, and I'll puff and I'll bloooooow your house down!'" Selena raised a hand and formed it into claws, then puffed her cheeks as she blew out gusts of air. The children around her gasped in fright but kept their attention on her.

Quinn suppressed a laugh at the irony of her reading *The Three Little Pigs* but stayed silent, leaning back on the bookshelves as he continued to watch Selena. A small pang tugged at his heart, seeing her surrounded by children. There was something so natural about it, and he suddenly had a vision of Selena holding a baby and maybe of her tucking a little girl into bed or kissing a boy's skinned knee.

The sounds of claps from the children shook him out of his

daydream. The parents and the children surrounded Selena, thanking her for the story, and she smiled at them gratefully, chatting with each one. Quinn waited until the small crowd started thinning before approaching her.

He was about to call her name when his throat went dry as his eyes were drawn to Selena's perfectly-shaped ass. She was bent over, picking up a discarded book on the floor, her heart-shaped backside covered in a pair of tight white slacks. The fact that there were no visible panty lines made him stifle a groan. "Hey," he managed to croak out.

Selena froze and slowly rose up, then turned around to face him. "What part of 'stay the hell away from me' don't you understand?" she asked, her eyes turning stormy.

"Selena, I'm sorry," he said. "Please, don't go." He grabbed her arm when she tried to walk away. The touch of her bare skin sent tingles up his arm, but he didn't let go. "Evie told me. I'm sorry Selena. I didn't mean ... I wasn't trying to insult you; you have to believe me." Shit, he was fucking this up.

Her shoulders sagged. "Fine. You've said sorry, you can leave now."

"I can't," he blurted out. "I mean, I have something for you. To say sorry." He fished an envelope out of his pocket and handed it to her. "Here." When she looked at him with narrowed eyes, he sighed. "It's not poison or a trick or whatever evil thing you're thinking. Just open it."

Selena took the envelope and opened it gingerly, peering inside. Her eyes widened. "What is this? How did you get this?" She took out the two pieces of paper. "The *Lord of the Rings* exhibit's been sold out for weeks, and it's ending on Sunday! How did you get tickets?"

"A friend owed me a favor." He shrugged. Actually, he had spent the whole night on various internet forums, trying to buy some tickets. When he couldn't even get those geeks to talk to him, he changed his screen name to 'sexyelf4447' and got flooded with offers. He shuddered at what some of those sick bastards wanted in exchange, but, finally, he got the tickets for a hefty sum.

"Wow, I didn't know you had real friends."

"Ha!" The old Selena was back, the one who wasn't mad at him for hurting her. Wolf finally calmed down, settling inside him. It had been just as anxious as he had been, waiting for her reaction. "So, am I forgiven?"

"Hmmm." She thought for a moment. "I suppose."

"Good." Finally, the tightness in his chest lightened. "Well, I guess I'll see you." He pivoted to leave, but her hand on his arm stopped him.

"Wait," she said.

"Huh?"

"Why don't you come with me?"

"What?" His voice croaked like he was some damned teen going through puberty. He did get her two tickets but figured she'd want to go with Evie or someone else. "I've never seen the movies, but sure. Let's go."

"Wait, now?" Selena frowned.

Jeez, now you scared her. "I mean, if you've been wanting to see the exhibit and it's sold out, then it'll probably be crowded this weekend since it's closing."

"True." She tapped her finger on her chin. "All right, I have to clock out, but I can leave now."

Quinn followed Selena to her desk, letting her walk a few steps ahead. She was wearing those spiky heels again with her white, high-waisted pants and a frilly blouse that brought out the blue in her eyes. She tucked away her reading glasses, but damn if the outfit didn't make him think of sexy librarian fantasies again. He swallowed hard as his eyes darted across the rows of books, imagining what he'd do if they were alone. Probably start by pushing her up against the shelves and then...*whoa there, cowboy*. What the fuck was he thinking? This was Selena, for Christ's sake.

"So, *Three Little Pigs*, huh?" he asked, trying to clear his mind.

She picked up her jacket and put it on. "I didn't choose it on purpose. I didn't even know you were watching, you creeper. Besides, didn't I make a convincing wolf?"

"Hmmm ... not bad, but you can use some work. You need more growling and bigger teeth, and wolves definitely don't blow houses down."

"Well, that's the point of the story," she said. "That the blowhard wolf loses in the end," she added with a twinkle in her eye.

He laughed. "These damn fairy tales. Always making the wolves the bad guys. Don't they know wolves can be good?"

"You'll have to take that up with the Brothers Grimm, I'm afraid. I only read them." She chuckled. "Okay, I'm ready."

They walked out of the library, and Quinn hailed a cab, despite Selena's protests that they could take the subway uptown. "My treat," he said. "For the hot dogs."

Neither spoke on the ride, but Quinn enjoyed the comfortable silence in the back of the yellow cab. As Selena looked out the window, Quinn watched her, tracing his sight along the milky skin of her cheeks, over the button nose and generous mouth, wondering how...fucking hell, get a hold of yourself. Maybe he did need to get laid if he was starting to think of her that way. A trip to Blood Moon tonight might do the trick.

The cab stopped abruptly, jolting Quinn out of his thoughts. He handed the cabbie some cash and followed Selena out of the vehicle. He couldn't help but notice how Selena seemed so excited. She was practically bouncing on her feet, and her mouth was forming into a smile as they approached the entrance to the exhibit.

"What kind of exhibit is this, anyway?" he asked.

"They're showcasing a bunch of stuff from the movies and the books," she explained. "They've got some really cool stuff. Props and costumes from the film and a couple of things from the Tolkien Estate—stuff that's never left England until now. The organizers received special permission to bring them to New York."

They gave their tickets to the attendant by the gate and walked into the exhibit.

"Oh! Let's start here!" Selena said excitedly, tugging his hand as she led him into one of the rooms.

Quinn watched Selena as she oohed and ahhed over the different displays in the various rooms. She was animated as she talked, not really letting Quinn get a word in edgewise, but he didn't mind as she seemed so happy, just talking about the different costumes and props and various items from the movies and the author himself. And seeing her in good spirits lightened his mood, too. Even Wolf was curled up contentedly inside him.

When they got to the door of the last room, she stopped and turned to him. "Now, we come to the best part. The reason why this exhibit is sold out." Her eyes sparkled as she drew the curtain aside and they stepped into the final exhibit.

It was dark inside, illuminated only by fairy lights placed all around the room. They seemed to be in a forest at night, surrounded by trees and shrubbery. Giant tree trunks rose around them, giving a feeling of being high up in the canopy of a forest. In the middle was an elaborately carved arch and a set of steps.

"It's ..."

"*Lothlorien*," Quinn finished.

"How did you know?" she asked, her jaw dropping. "I thought you said you've never seen the movies?"

"I told you I read," he said smugly. "I've read all the books a couple of times. I didn't want to see the movies because I had this vision in my head and didn't want to ruin it." He looked around. "Hmmm ... not bad."

Selena snorted. "They recreated the entire set from the movie in here. I think it deserves more than a 'not bad.'" She walked up the steps, her gaze transfixed on the delicately carved arches, examining the details.

Quinn thought it really was amazing, and aside from a few details here and there, it was close to what he had imagined all those years ago when he first read the book while huddled in one of Archie's leather armchairs. However, even the amazing set couldn't stop him from glancing at Selena and he watched her face look up in wonder. The lights were illuminating her beautiful face with an unearthly glow. Her blue-gray eyes glittered and her pink lips parted, and he suddenly found himself right behind her, taking in her yummy butterscotch scent.

"Did you see the—oomph!" Selena turned around, not realizing how close he was, and bumped right into him. To prevent her from falling back, he wrapped his arms around her and brought her close to his chest.

"Hey now, klutz," he said. "Watch where you're going."

"Me?" she asked in an incredulous voice. "What the hell are you doing, anyway, standing right behind me?"

"I was trying to get a better view."

"There's no one else here," she pointed out. "Now will you please ..." She tried to squirm out of his arms, but Quinn tightened his grip around her. "Just let go."

Quinn wasn't sure what possessed him, maybe it was *Lothlorien* or Wolf's happy groans and sighs, but he leaned his head down and planted his mouth on hers. The touch of their lips sent a shock of electricity and something alien through his system. Selena let out a surprised squeak, but soon melted into his arms. Her soft curves pressed up against his body felt *so right*, but, at the same time, sent fear straight to his gut.

"Ahem."

They quickly broke apart as a stern-faced older woman stood in front of them, her hand on her hip and her gaze steely. Behind her, a group of kids was staring at them, wide-eyed. Someone in the back giggled, and, soon, all the children followed suit, much to their teacher's chagrin.

"Uh, sorry," Quinn apologized quickly. He took Selena's hand and dragged her out of the exhibit, into the main hallway.

"What the hell was that about?" she hissed, snatching her hand away.

"Yeah, who brings kids to a *Lord of the Rings* exhibit, anyway?"

"That's not what I meant!" she replied, her voice lowering to a whisper as more people passed by them, the exhibit reaching its peak time. "You ... we ... you can't just do that!"

The anger in her voice sent a pang of hurt to his chest, but he swallowed it down and did what he always did when he felt like this. He let out a laugh. "Do what, kitten?" he asked, flashing her lopsided smile.

"Kiss me, you idiot!"

"You mean, here?" he asked. "In front of all these people? I don't know ... you should probably take me out to dinner first."

"You're such an ass! I mean, you can't kiss me like that!"

"Sheesh, lighten up, Selena," he shot back. "It was just a kiss, no big deal." Wolf, on the other hand, thought it was a very big deal and was urging him to do it again, but he told the thing to shut the hell up. "Besides, it's not like you were fighting me off."

"How could I when your steroid-jacked arms were keeping me from moving?"

"I'll have you know that these guns," he said, pointing to his arms, "are all natural. No 'roids needed."

She let out a sigh. "Never mind. It was a terrible kiss, anyway."

"What?" he exclaimed. What the fuck was she saying? He was a good kisser, and he had a trail of happy women to prove it. He was about to protest when he saw the glint in her eyes. "You're fucking with me!"

"Lighten up, Quinn, it was just a kiss, no big deal," she laughed and then slapped him playfully in the arm. "Let's just forget it, okay? We got caught up in the magic of Tolkien, that was it."

"Yeah," he said weakly. "That's it." He squared his shoulders. "This would never work between us anyway."

"Of course not," Selena said.

Her agreement came a little too quickly for his taste, but he pressed on. "I'm not looking for a relationship, you know. Too many complications, and women only want one thing."

"And what is that?" she asked, her brows raised.

"You know, to trap us men into marriage, commitment, kids. The whole shebang."

"Right. Because you're such good husband material," she said dryly. "Well, I don't need a relationship either and certainly not one with you."

"We're in agreement then." He stuck out his hand. "No relationship for us."

She shook it. "Yeah, definitely not."

"So, we should just stay friends."

"Yes, we should." She nodded, then frowned. "Wait, were we friends before?"

"We were ... whatever we were. Now, even though you're a nerd and you're short, I think we can be friends."

"And even though you're a jackass, the fact that you read Tolkien has earned you a smidgen of respect in my book, so I guess we can be friends."

"Good," he agreed. "Now, let's go get some dinner because I'm starving."

4

*A*fter the exhibit, she and Quinn had dinner at a Mexican place a few blocks away. They spent most of the meal throwing insults at each other and laughing, and, though she had a good time, she couldn't wait to get home.

As Selena closed the door to her apartment, she breathed out a long sigh. Now that she could let her guard down, all the tension left her body, and she slumped back against the front door. Her knees buckled at the memory of that kiss. Quinn's lips had sent desire straight to her belly (and if she was really honest, much lower), but, apparently, it was all a joke to Quinn.

The sting of rejection had hit her hard, although she really should have been used to it by now. But still, coming from him, it hurt. So, she put on her usual front—brassy, bold, and completely unfazed. She was just "one of the guys" because, as she learned growing up, it hurt less. It meant not having to worry that her stepsisters would go after a boy the moment Selena showed interest in him. It also meant it was easier to pretend it didn't hurt when a guy dropped her like a hot potato the moment either Alexis or Katrina started paying attention to him.

She told herself it was better this way. On looks alone, Quinn was way out of her league. It took all her strength not to melt whenever he flashed her those baby blues or to keep staring at his full mouth. The feel of it on hers branded into her brain. Today, he was wearing another one of those too-tight shirts that showed off his perfect physique and those ripped jeans that molded to his ass.

"I'm such an idiot," she said aloud, slamming her fists on the door. With another loud sigh, she walked over to the couch and plopped down, sinking into the cushions. Why did she invite him to go to the exhibit anyway? Sure, it was sweet of him to get her those tickets, but he didn't even assume he would go with her. She should have just said thanks and let him go.

A buzzing sound snapped Selena out of her thoughts, and she grabbed her phone, checking the caller ID—*Dad*. She let out another groan. She'd been dodging her father's calls for days now.

Tossing the phone aside, she grabbed one of the throw pillows and placed it over her face. She let out a muffled scream as she waited for the call to go to voicemail.

If only Quinn had been his usual asshole self during dinner. Sure, they traded barbs, but he was so sweet. He even pulled out her chair for her, asked her what she wanted to eat, and then paid for the meal. For Christ's sake, he even brought her back to her apartment in Washington Heights, even though he lived in the opposite direction, and waited until she was safely in the building before leaving. It was frustrating because her heart did little flip-flops whenever he smiled at her. She had to repeat his words in her head over and over again to tell the damn thing to stop. Quinn was not a relationship type of guy. From the moment they met, she branded him a manwhore, and he confirmed it today. But what about her? Well, that was complicated.

Her phone beeped, indicating a message had come in. Wow, a call followed by a message. Her father was serious. She picked up the phone from between the cushions and glanced at the text. *Call me.* Another long sigh. She supposed she couldn't put it off. Hitting the return call button, she braced herself.

"Hi, Dad."

"Selena," Leonard Merlin replied. "Why didn't you pick up?"

"I was ... in the bathroom."

"All right, well, I've been trying to get a hold of you the entire week."

"I know, I'm sorry dad. Things are busy at work. Budget cuts and all," she lied.

"Well, now that I have your undivided attention," Leonard began, "We need to talk."

"About what?"

"Joseph and Melissa want to formalize your engagement to Jason. A summer solstice wedding would be a good omen and who knows, maybe by this time next year, you'll have my grandchild."

"Er ..." Oh yeah, that's what was complicated.

Few people outside the magical world knew how their society worked. The amount of power a witch or warlock had dictated their place in the hierarchy of things, and Selena, being powerless, had no social standing at all. No warlock should have wanted her, but being distantly related to Charlotte Fontaine (the most powerful witch in their history) and her last name somehow gave her an edge and made her a better prospect than even Alexis or Katrina. While she may be Selena the Dud, there was a chance her children could come into power, and even blessed power. Witch and warlock marriages weren't strictly arranged, certain pairings were encouraged, especially if both parties wanted to secure their position in the magical community.

Selena initially didn't want to marry anyone at all. Having been burned so many times by past crushes falling for her stepsisters, she was holding out and hoping they would settle down first. But her father had been insistent, telling her if she wanted to have children with any power at all, her only chance was with a powerful warlock. She was actually surprised to learn that Jason Ward, the son of one of their elders, had any interest in her. Not only was he a talented warlock, but his father was also one of the more prominent coven elders. She'd known Jason since grade school and though they'd been in some classes together in high school, it wasn't like they were best friends. In fact, he seemed rather cold, not just to her but to everyone. She knew Alexis and Katrina both had their eyes on him, but he didn't take their bait, a fact that had her stepsisters steaming mad.

It was just after Christmas when her father told her Jason was interested. Frankly, she was surprised, but Jason came to her in person and put it so logically. They were both relatively young, which meant they could try for a couple of kids. Jason was a partner in his father's law firm, and she could stay home and raise the children if she wanted to. Really, if she was going into an arrangement, she couldn't have asked for a better person. Jason said she could take her time to consider his proposal. But still, she thought of him like a stranger, even though she'd known him her whole life. How could she muster up any lust for him? Thoughts of lust brought back memories of Quinn and their kiss. Talk about bad timing.

"Selena, are you there?"

How long had she zoned out? Selena rubbed her eyes. "Yes, I'm here, Dad."

"So, what about it?" Leonard asked. "We can have the engagement party at Glenwood. Melissa says she'll take care of everything, and all you have to do is show up."

"I don't know, dad."

There was silence on the line for what seemed like forever. "Selena. How could you possibly need more time to think about this? Don't you see that this is your only chance to make a good match? Jason Ward could have any witch he wants, but he chose you."

"I—"

"Selena, you won't be able to find a better offer than this. In fact, I highly doubt any warlock with even a smidgen of power would be interested in you. Can't you see? This is your duty. To help produce the next generation of witches and warlocks. Don't you want children?"

Selena bit her lip. Of course she wanted kids. She would love any child she had, magical or not, but if they were magical, it would make their lives easier. Unlike hers. "You can't possibly expect me to marry someone I don't know."

Leonard let out a laugh and then his voice turned serious. "Really, Selena, how can you be so choosy? I swear, if you don't give this some serious thought ... there will be consequences."

Her father's voice cut deep into her. Leonard didn't have to say it, but she knew what that meant. When her mother was alive, she was always telling Selena the importance of being part of the community, and, while she was growing up, she did enjoy coven life. It was only when she hit puberty and her powers didn't come in that they started treating her differently. Not cruelly, the way her stepsisters did, but they all gave her looks of pity, and she knew they all thought the same thing—what a shame that a child from two powerful bloodlines turned out to be a disappointment. Still, the coven was important to her and to the memory of her mother.

If Leonard was saying what she thought he was saying, it meant only one thing. Banishment. She'd be shunned instead of pitied. No support system. She wouldn't even be able to visit Philadelphia or her childhood home or her mother's grave.

"I ... fine ..." she relented. "I'll think about it some more and give him my answer soon." Not like she had any other prospects anyway. Maybe she should consider the engagement.

"Good. I'll be waiting to hear your decision." And with that, her father hung up.

In truth, Selena had all but forgotten about Jason's proposal in the last few weeks. At that time, she had not only been flattered but considered it. She wanted a child and a family, but her stepsisters seemed determined to make sure no man would come near her. But now? The thought of marrying Jason made her stomach churn, which was strange. She wasn't disgusted, but it just seemed ... wrong. And then, of course, there was the other part. Sex.

Selena didn't want to die alone, surrounded by the cats she would surely have hoarded by the time she went senile, and have her body discovered by a neighbor when her corpse began to stink up the hallway. And she didn't want to die a virgin, either. Alexis and Katrina stole every single boy in high school who even showed a margin of interest in her, so she never had a boyfriend or even a friend-with-benefits. And, with Alexis following her to the same college she didn't even bother. Instead, she focused all her time and energy on graduating with honors so she could get the hell out of Philadelphia.

The door unlocking and opening caught her attention, and she sat up straight, trying to look casual.

"Hey Evie-girl," she said as the brunette entered the apartment.

"Hey Sel," Evie replied. She dropped her things in the small foyer and walked over to the couch, plopping down beside her.

"How was your day?"

"Ugh." Evie slumped back and put an arm over her eyes. "I swear, I'm never going to get a callback."

"Don't worry. It'll happen." Selena had been to many of Evie's open mic nights, and she knew her best friend was incredibly talented. Evie just needed one break, and once people saw her on stage, she'd finally reach her dream of becoming a famous Broadway actress.

"Yeah, well, I'm just glad I have a paying job now, and I can stay here," she said. "How about you? Anything interesting happen?"

Yeah, a hot Lycan kissed me, and my father threatened to banish me if I didn't get into an arranged marriage. "You know, same old, same old." Pushing thoughts of the day aside, she linked her arm through Evie's. "C'mon, let's go spend time with our best boyfriends."

Evie giggled. "You mean Ben and Jerry?"

"I have that emergency carton stashed in the back," Selena said. "I have a feeling tonight's as good a time as any to break it out."

5

*Q*uinn shut down his computer after he sent the last email to Sebastian, then proceeded to lock up the office. With Killian gone on his honeymoon, a lot of the extra work had fallen on his shoulders, but he didn't mind. Most of the work he did for Lone Wolf was background stuff, and if he could pitch in so his brother could have some quality time with his bride, he was happy to help. Besides, once the baby arrived, Killian and Luna could say goodbye to alone time. *Suckers.* Sure, the couple was ecstatic about the baby, and he liked his new sister-in-law enough, but Quinn still couldn't wrap his head around why anyone would have kids. For Lycans, the answer was easy though. Shifters had difficulty producing, and any Lycan who had a kid with a non-Lycan always produced a human child, with the exception of True Mates, which Killian and Luna were. Still, there was no way Quinn was going to knock anyone up accidentally, and even though it was unlikely he'd ever impregnate any girl and Lycans didn't get diseases, he always made sure to wear protection.

A pain slashed at him, and Wolf was once again antsy because it knew he would be thinking of the past. No, he would never knock up some girl and leave her high and dry. Growing up with a single mom, he knew what that meant, and he swore to himself that he would never be like the father he never knew.

For some reason, his thoughts strayed to Selena, and that seemed to calm Wolf down. He wondered what she was up to after their dinner last night. As soon as he dropped Selena off at home, Quinn went straight to Blood Moon, hoping some alcohol or a pretty face could help him forget about that afternoon. Selena's lips, smell, and the memory of her curves against his body seemed to be all he could think about, and he just wanted to get her out of his mind. He tried flirting with this blonde Lycan by the bar, but she wasn't having it. She could probably sense Wolf, how agitated it was, and she stayed as far away from him as possible. He thought about walking up to a group of college girls, humans for sure, but that left a bad taste in his mouth. After another beer, he went home, alone and frustrated, with nothing to sate him except his damn hand.

After closing up the office, Quinn had meant to walk back to his loft in Soho, but somehow, for the third day in a row, he found himself entering the doors of the Lower Manhattan Library.

Selena was at her desk, as usual, face scrunched up in concentration. Her wild red hair was piled up in a bun, held together by a pencil. She was wearing her reading glasses and chewing on the end of a pen. The way her lips wrapped around the shaft made him stifle a groan. He never wanted to be a pen so badly in his life.

"Selena," he called, making her jump in surprise.

"Jesus H. Christ," she yelped, holding her hand to her chest, the pen dropping from her lips. "You damned Lycans and your super stealth." She took a deep breath, her eyes darting around. "What are you doing here?"

"Well, I was hungry ..."

"This is a library, not a restaurant," she retorted, turning back to her computer. "Go get some pizza or something."

"Great idea," he replied. "Get your coat, and we can grab a slice at this great place—"

She whipped her head back to him. "Excuse me?"

He pointed at the clock with his chin. "It's past five. You should clock out so you can go and have dinner with me."

She raised a brow at him. "Dinner with you?"

"Yeah, you know, me. Your friend. Just a quick slice." He emphasized the friend part, hoping that would convince her. Selena seemed skittish today, like she would bolt at any moment, and he didn't know why.

"Right." She sat there, staring at the screen.

"Well?" he asked impatiently.

She shrugged. "Fine. Let me close up, and we can go."

"Great," he said. "Hurry up. I'm starving."

Selena rolled her eyes, but a smile tugged at the corner of her lips. When she finished closing up her station, she followed him out the door. They walked a few blocks uptown until they reached the edge of Little Italy and a red brick building on a quiet corner of the neighborhood.

"I heard this place has the best pizza in the city," Quinn said as he opened the door for her. "They're originally from Brooklyn, but they just opened this branch."

"Mama Jean's?" Selena looked up at the sign over the door. "I've heard of them. The lines there are insane."

"Yeah, good thing they're still doing a soft opening here and the word hasn't spread yet." He walked up to the counter. "Go ahead and take a seat. I'll get us a pie."

"I thought you said we were going for a quick slice?"

"I'll get you a soda, too," he said, ignoring her protest. "What do you want on your half?"

"Fine," Selena said. "Hawaiian."

Quinn gave her a thumbs up and then ordered at the counter. He grabbed their drinks and sat down across from her at the table she reserved.

"You know, they say there are two kinds of people in the world," Quinn said as he set the tray on the table. "Those who don't eat pineapple on their pizza and monsters."

"Oh, ha ha," she mocked. "Not like I've never heard that one before."

"So, how was your day?" Quinn asked.

She sighed. "Just the usual ..."

As Selena told Quinn about her day, he watched, engrossed in what she had to say. He listened intently, thankful for his ability to multi-task because he couldn't help but notice the way her eyes lit up and her hands moved around when she was excited. A tendril of hair had escaped from her makeshift bun, brushing her cheek, and he itched to touch it and put it behind her ear.

"So, what about you?" she asked. "What sorts of things have you been up to? Anything you can talk about?"

"Just been working on a few cases here and there," he said.

"Like what?"

"You really want to know?

"Yeah, sure," she said.

"Well, right now we've been concentrating on reuniting some Lone Wolves with their families." Quinn recounted the story of how the mages had created an army of Lone Wolves to help them with their plan to destroy the clans. When the battle was over, and they won, Grant Anderson, the Alpha of New York, took the Lone Wolves in to try and rehabilitate them and possibly find out if they still had living relatives. "It's taking a while because few of them can remember what happened before they became Lone Wolves. Most of them were kids when they lost their clans."

"What about you?"

"Huh?"

Selena looked up at him curiously with her blue-gray eyes. "I mean, do you remember what life was like before you became a Lone Wolf?"

"No," he lied. "All I remember is Archie, my adoptive father. He took me, Killian, Connor, and Meredith in when he suspected that the mages were trying to build their army."

"You must remember something," Selena pressed. "Aren't you curious?"

"Not at all." Underneath the table, his fingers curled tightly. He took a breath, willing the memories not to come to the surface. His mother's face, so faint now in his mind's eye, swam back to his conscious mind. Anna, he thought. That was her name. She worked as a waitress to support her and Quinn. He remembered the small apartment they lived in, the Murphy bed they shared, and how tired she looked after a long day at work. How his clothes were threadbare because they could only shop at the thrift stores. The other kids at school laughed at him, and when he came home crying, asking why they were so poor and why he didn't have a dad, Anna was on the verge of tears as she told him the truth. He was eight years old.

"Quinn?" Selena asked, concern marring her face. "Are you all right?" She slid her hand over to his. Her palm was warm and sent a soothing calm over him. Before he could answer, the waiter arrived with their pizza, and he gave a silent sigh of relief.

As soon as the food was on their plates, they dug in. Selena was definitely not one of those women who was afraid to eat in front of a man; in fact, she polished off two huge slices without even batting an eye. Normally, if he were taking some chick out, she'd order a salad and end up pushing most of it around her plate. God, had he been dating the same types of girls all this time?

He looked down at the pie, realizing the empty plates meant that their meal was almost done. "So, I was thinking, if what I saw at the exhibit last night was the set from the movie, I'm ready to watch the films."

"Really?" she asked. "That's great! You'll be in for a treat! You have to tell me what you think."

"Well, why don't you watch it with me?"

"Huh?"

"Yeah," he continued. "You're the reason I went to that exhibit in the first place, so you should pop my movie cherry."

Unfortunately, at that exact moment, Selena had been taking a drink out of her glass, and she began to choke, spitting soda all over the table.

"I ... ugh ... Oh God ..."

Quinn smirked, shook his head and handed her a napkin. "Sheesh, I can't take you anywhere, can I?"

Selena coughed and wiped her face with the napkin. "Sorry, I was just ... uh ..." She gave a nervous laugh. "Seriously, though? It's a movie, not a life changing event. You don't need me to be there to hold your hand, you know."

"Yeah, well I bet you have all the movies on DVD."

She grew quiet. "Blu-Ray. Extended edition."

"Ha! I knew it, nerd. Now," he said, pushing his chair back. "I know this is going to be a four-hour affair, so maybe if we leave for your place now, we can finish before midnight."

*S*elena didn't protest when he suggested they watch the movie at her place. In fact, she was insistent they watch it on Blu-Ray instead of streaming, so he could get the full effect since he didn't get a chance to watch it in the theater.

They took a cab to her apartment, which took a while since

she lived all the way up in Washington Heights. The neighborhood itself was lively, but she lived on a quiet street facing the East River. It was an older building, but it seemed secure enough. His instinct was to check for dangers and security weaknesses, after all, and he was satisfied with what he saw. Of course, with two girls living on their own, he told himself it was only natural for him to worry.

He followed her into the building and up the stairs to the second floor. Selena opened the door to the apartment and let him in.

"Nice place," he observed. By New York standards, it was spacious. There was a small foyer that led into a kitchen, and, to his right, he could see the living room from behind a sheer curtain. It was bright, airy, and feminine; precisely the type of place he imagined Selena would have.

"Yeah, the rent's pretty decent for Manhattan, but the commute to downtown sucks," she said as she hung her jacket on the coat rack. "Go ahead and make yourself comfortable. Want some snacks or drinks?"

"Sure," he replied and walked into the spacious living room. The couch was quite large and comfortable, and there was a 40-inch TV on a media console on the other end of the living room. The space was decorated tastefully and there were books everywhere, lining the shelves, on stacks in the corners, and even on the coffee table. "You live here with Evie?"

"Yeah," she said as she set a tray with drinks down on the coffee table. "That's the bedroom; we have twin beds in there." She nodded at the door down a small hallway.

"You don't mind sharing?"

She laughed. "Nah, it's like having a sister I actually like. And it helps with the rent and expenses. Anyway, the popcorn's in the microwave, and I'll set the movie up." Selena walked to the media shelf and picked up a case, took out a disc, and then slid it into the player. She walked to the kitchen and, minutes later, came out with a huge bowl of popcorn.

Selena grabbed the remote and pressed play. "Okay, let's start," she said, plopping down beside him and placing the bowl between them.

The credits began to play, and then the prologue began. Quinn was enjoying himself, despite his initial misgivings about watching the movie. Of course, he would also glance at Selena every now and then, from the corner of his eye. She'd probably seen the movies millions of times, but she remained transfixed, reacting to every scene as if she were seeing it for the first time.

About halfway through the movie, Quinn heard a key slip into the lock and turn, followed by the opening of the door.

"I'm home!" Evie greeted. "What are you—Quinn?"

"Hey, Evie," he said.

"What are you doing here?"

"We're watching a movie," he answered. "Duh."

"I can see that." The brunette eyed him suspiciously and crossed her arms over her chest. "I mean, what are you doing watching it here? In my apartment."

"Yours and Selena's," he reminded her. "She invited me."

"Wait, you invited Quinn to watch a movie here?" Evie asked.

"Yeah," Selena mumbled, her eyes never leaving the screen.

"But—"

"Shhh, this is my favorite part!" she cried. "The Mines of Moria!"

Evie rolled her eyes. "You watch this movie once a month."

Selena ignored her friend and shoved a handful of popcorn into her mouth.

Evie let out a long-suffering sigh. "I'm heading to bed. I'm exhausted." She waved to Quinn and disappeared into the bedroom.

They continued to watch the movie, though he could tell she was getting sleepy by her droopy eyelids. She continued to fight it though, forcing her eyes open, trying to stay awake. Near the end of the movie, Selena had lost. Her eyes completely shut and she slumped forward. He moved to catch her, his arms going around her and hauling her back, which only resulted in her falling on top of him.

Quinn took in a full whiff of her sweet scent as his nose buried in her hair. Her soft, pliant body pressed against him, and her full, large breasts flattened on his chest. She pushed her face into the crook of his neck, murmuring softly, but she seemed to remain asleep. He stifled a groan, feeling all the blood from his brain go straight to his cock.

He was only glad she was asleep because Quinn wasn't sure what he'd do if she were awake and on top of him. Her wild mane had long escaped the bun and fell in unruly waves down her back, tickling the skin on his arms. He lifted a hand and touched her cheek, observing the light dusting of freckles on the bridge of her nose. Selena was gorgeous; he had always thought so, from the first moment he laid eyes on her. Even if she did call him a "rude fuck," he couldn't help but be drawn to her.

Wolf was going crazy, urging him on. To do what, he didn't know. Maybe taste her lips again or lie down on the couch and roll over on top of her, just to see how the curves of her body fit against his.

God, he was going insane. That was the only explanation. Sure, Selena was attractive, but she wasn't his usual type. Well, the big boobs were exactly his type. But the things he felt when she was around scared him shitless. Besides, Evie was her best friend. If things went badly (and knowing his track record, they probably would) and their admin assistant quit, Killian would murder him, and God knows what Connor would do.

With a resigned sigh, he disentangled Selena's arms and laid her back on the couch. She stirred and moaned, but didn't wake up. He found a throw blanket on the loveseat and put it over her, tucking it under her chin. What was it about Selena that made it hard for him to turn away and leave her alone? He would have to do it. Avoid her and forget about her.

He let himself out the door, closing it behind him and making sure the lock clicked before he left.

6

*S*elena smoothed down her skirt and checked her lipstick for what seemed like the millionth time that day on the glass of Lone Wolf Security's door. Evie was scheduled to work at the office today, which was why Selena came around. *Yup, that was totally the reason why.* And it was also a nice, sunny day, which was why she wore her favorite blue-gray dress that matched her eyes and showed off her legs. Plus, she woke up feeling refreshed and had time to fix her hair, taming it into glossy curls down her back. Yes, that was the reason she was standing outside Quinn's office, not feeling nervous at all. Straightening her spine, Selena knocked on the door and waited for it to open.

"Selena! It's nice to see you again!" Luna Rhoades, Killian's wife, greeted her.

Behind her, sitting on the couch, was a blond woman Selena recognized as Meredith, Quinn's adopted sister and the only female member of their family. "Selena! Long time, no see."

"Hi, Meredith, Luna," she said, surprised to see both women as she stepped inside the office. "You're back. How was the honeymoon?"

Luna blushed. "Amazing. We went to this private island in the Caribbean that the Alpha owns."

Selena whistled. "Private island, huh? Sounds nice! And it looks like you got some tanning done! Naked hopefully?"

"Well, there was lots of naked time …"

"Eww, no details please," Meredith said, sticking her fingers in her ears.

Selena laughed. "Wow, I'm surprised." She looked down at Luna's pregnant belly, and she estimated she was six months along now. "But, you go girl! Glad you got some!" She raised her hand, and Luna heartily high-fived her.

"Pregnancy hormones, don't you know?" Meredith quipped, rubbing her own pregnant belly.

"Good thing that's not contagious," Selena joked as she sat next to Meredith.

"Are you here for lunch?" Luna asked.

"Uh-huh." Selena looked around. "Where's Evie?"

"She's in the office with Killian and Quinn, just giving him a rundown of what happened while we were away."

As if on cue, Killian, Quinn, and Evie walked out of the office.

"I'll get that done for you, Boss, no worries," Evie said brightly. "Oh, hey Selena!"

"Hey Evie!" she greeted back and nodded at the two men behind her. "Killian. Quinn." She tried to keep her voice as even as possible, but Quinn and his damned smile were making her heart thud loudly against her ribcage.

"Hey, Selena," Quinn said.

"Hello, Selena," Killian said as he walked to his wife. He put a hand on her shoulder. "Lunch with Evie, right?"

"Uh-huh."

"Well, have a good one. We have to be off for a meeting at Fenrir Corp."

Luna frowned and let out a sigh. "We're not going home yet?"

"Sorry, sweetheart. It was unexpected, but the Alpha could only meet us today," Killian said. "Are you feeling sick?"

"It's just ..." she sighed. "It's getting harder to move around, you know, and I don't want to get stuck in the Alpha's waiting room while you have your meeting."

"I'm sorry." Killian let out a deep breath. "Maybe we can reschedule."

"Don't be silly, Killian," Meredith interjected. "Why don't you boys get to your meeting and come back here to pick up Luna? We can all stay in and have lunch here."

"Sounds like a plan," Luna said. "Do you mind?"

"Not at all, sweetheart." Killian leaned down and kissed his wife on the forehead, then patted her belly affectionately. "I'll be back. Quinn," he called. "Let's go."

"Yeah, sure," Quinn shrugged. "See you, girls." His eyes flickered to Selena briefly before he left. She stared at them, her eyes transfixed on the door as it shut. When she woke up this morning, she was disappointed that she was all alone. The only evidence he had been there at all was his delicious aftershave that seemed to linger in the air. He had been so sweet the whole night, watching the movie with her. And he had tucked her in, too.

"Selena Merlin!" Evie exclaimed, jolting her out of her reverie. "Oh no. Don't you dare!"

"What?" She gave Evie her best "who me?" look.

"Girl, I'm warning you!"

"What's going on?" Meredith asked.

Selena's eyes darted from Evie to Meredith. "No, don't *you* dare."

"Quinn was over at our place last night," Evie said smugly. "Snuggling on the couch with Selena."

"We were not snuggling!" Selena protested. "Are you getting back at me for what I told them about the night you met Connor?"

"Shut. The. Front. Door." Meredith shot to her feet, a miracle considering her advanced pregnancy. "You were making out with Quinn? At your house?"

"We were not making out!" Selena corrected. "We were just watching *Fellowship of the Ring*."

"Was it a date?" Luna asked.

"It was not a date. We are not dating," Selena said. "We had dinner and then watched the movie."

"Sounds like a date to me," Evie said, crossing her arms and raising a brow at her.

"It was a ... friend date," she said, emphasizing the friend part.

"I didn't know you and Quinn were *friends* now," Meredith retorted. "You guys are always at each other's throats."

"Are you sleeping with him?" Evie asked.

"Jesus, Evie, no," Selena answered.

"Really, now?"

"I'm not sleeping with Quinn. I've never even slept with anyone!" She slapped her hand over her mouth as three pairs of eyes zeroed in on her.

Evie was the first to react. "Wait ... Selena ... you're a ..."

"Yes, I'm a virgin!" she blurted out. "Jeez, you guys should see yourselves. You all look like you've never seen a virgin before."

"It's just that ... you know ..."

"What? You think someone like me couldn't possibly be a virgin?"

"Well, yes," Evie replied.

"What the hell does that mean?" Selena huffed.

"I mean, look at you." Evie waved her hand up and down.

"Selena—news flash—you're gorgeous. Guys are always checking you out."

"What?" Selena looked at her strangely. "No guys look at me."

"Are you blind?" Meredith added. "There are lots of guys totally into you. I mean, your tits alone are enough to launch a thousand ships."

"Meredith," Luna warned.

"What?" The Lycan shrugged. "They are. Hey, if I batted for the other team, I'd be all over you. Why have you never bumped uglies with some hot dude? I thought you liked going to male strip clubs. And you were drooling all over Dante Muccino that time we ate at his restaurant."

"Well, I guess you can say I'm all talk," Selena said with a sigh. "And I don't know ... it just never seemed like the right time. I've never even had a boyfriend before."

"And you want to sleep with Quinn?" Evie asked. "Talk about bad ideas."

"Excuse me?" Selena shot back. "I'm supposed to be taking dating advice from *you*?"

Evie's shoulders sank in defeat. "You're right. I shouldn't be the one talking, considering the asshole parade that is my love life."

"It's all right, Evie," Luna said. "We've all been there. I'm sure between all of us, we could fill an entire book of assholes. I'll start: Chapter One, cheated on me while I was at a business conference."

"Chapter Two," Meredith added. "Slept with me to get back at his ex."

"Chapter Three," Evie said. "Texted me '*It's me, not you*' and then started dating my best friend the next day."

"Chapter Four," Luna continued. "Had a girlfriend."

"Chapter Five," Evie added. "Had a *boyfriend*."

"Really?" Meredith asked.

Evie shrugged. "I'm into theater. It was bound to happen."

"Chapter Six, has mommy issues," Luna giggled.

"Chapter Seven—"

"All right, all right, I get it," Selena added. "Men are awful, and I should be glad I stayed away from them."

"Look, Selena, it's not that you should stay away from guys entirely," Evie said. "I'm just saying ... be careful."

"I'm not going to sleep with Quinn. It's not like that. He doesn't want a relationship, and he's made that clear."

"Do you want to? Boink him, I mean."

Meredith's question caught her off guard, and when Selena didn't answer fast enough, the blond Lycan let out a laugh. "*Oh my God*. You do."

"I don't!" she said defensively. "Besides, you guys have to remember there's another party in the equation. Even if I wanted to sleep with him—which I don't—Quinn doesn't want me. He said so himself. He doesn't even find me attractive. I just ... ugh, my lunch hour's going to be over soon, and I haven't even eaten yet. I'm gonna grab a sandwich or something and head back to the library."

"Aww, don't go, Selena," Meredith pleaded. "We won't talk about you and Quinn anymore."

"Just ... don't rush into anything, okay?" Evie said.

"Jeez, *Mom*, I won't. Are you going to give me the sex talk, too?"

"I can give you the sex talk, if you want," Meredith offered.

"Uh, no thanks," Selena said. "So, food?"

"How about Chinese?" Evie asked. "I'm sure we could get Emerald Dragon to send over enough food to satisfy two pregnant women."

"Sounds great," Selena said, hoping the subject of sex and Quinn was finally going to be put to rest. Truth be told, the realization that Quinn was not interested in her like that stung. But that's what he'd been telling her all along, right? He said—after that goddamn kiss—he didn't do relationships or commitment. Of course he wouldn't be interested in that kind of stuff. Quinn was attractive, and he probably slept with a different girl each night. The thought of him slinking into some girl's bed after he left her last night sent a stab of jealousy through her, but she pushed it deep down inside. She should listen to her friends.

"Hello, Earth to Selena," Meredith said, waving her hand at Selena.

"Huh?"

"I was asking if you wanted fried rice or noodles."

"Uh, yes. I mean, rice, please."

Meredith raised a brow at her but said nothing. Thank goodness there wasn't any alcohol around, or she really would have been spilling her guts.

7

"So, you think some of the Lone Wolves are ready to be reunited with their families?" Killian asked Grant Anderson, Alpha of New York, as they sat in his office for their meeting.

"Dr. Faulkner's been doing some work with them, and I've also hired a very good psychologist," Grant replied. "They both agree that there are a few candidates who might be ready. How are we on locating their families?"

"Quinn's been working on finding them based on the interviews we conducted and facial recognition software," Killian said. "Quinn, let us know what you have. Quinn. Quinn?"

"For fuck's sake, are you with us?" Sebastian snapped at Quinn.

"Huh?" Quinn started, looking at the three men staring at him. Killian seemed curious, while Sebastian Creed looked annoyed. The Alpha, on the other hand, had a confused look on his face. "Yeah, sorry. Late night, you know."

"Gotta keep those women happy, right?" Killian joked.

"You do what you want on your own time," Sebastian

growled. "But when you're on the job, you keep your head straight."

"All right, all right," Quinn huffed, wondering why the hell Creed kept him around if he hated his guts. Sure, he made a bad impression on the boss when he hit on his mate the first time they met, but he thought that was in the past now. He shrugged. "Anyway, yeah, I've been working on the info we have and cross referenced it with the Lycan High Council files of shifters around the world. I've compiled a list of possible remaining family members for most of them, and I can grab addresses once we're ready." He took out his pad and handed it to Grant. The Alpha took it and began to swipe through the files.

"This is good work," Grant said. "You put all this together, just from the interviews from the Lone Wolves?"

"We didn't have much to work with," Quinn said. "Most of them had spotty memories; some don't even remember their real names or how old they are. I had to guesstimate for the most part and used some de-aging software to try and see what they would look like at different ages. Then it was a matter of figuring out how to get the information we needed."

"Excellent work." Grant looked at Sebastian. "I should have snapped up your Lone Wolves before you did, Creed. You're good at spotting talent. I bet Quinn here could have made millions in my tech department."

Sebastian laughed. "Yeah, well next time, don't be so slow, old man."

Grant chuckled. "I'll try to keep up with you whippersnappers. Now," he stood up, "I have a teleconference in five minutes. Would you mind showing yourselves out?"

"Not at all Alpha," Killian said, standing up. The three men left the office and headed to the private elevators that would take them to the garage.

"Next time we're in there, you stay focused," Sebastian told

Quinn when they were alone inside the elevator car. "I know you like to screw everything that moves, but think about pussy on your own time."

Quinn felt the anger boil inside of him at the insinuation, but Killian shot him a warning look. "Yeah, yeah. You're just jealous because you're both boring old married men now."

Sebastian's eyes narrowed, and Quinn felt the rumbling of the beast inside the other man. Shit. Well, it was a nice life. Good thing Killian's here and can identify the ashes. However, instead of turning into a giant dragon, Sebastian did something unexpected. He laughed.

Killian and Quinn looked at each other, confused.

"Motherfucker," Sebastian chuckled. "You weren't thinking about getting your dick stroked. You're thinking about a girl. *The girl.*"

"What?" Quinn exclaimed.

"So, Quinn," Killian snickered. "Who is she?"

"Forget what I said, you're not boring old married men," Quinn muttered. "You're more like old women who love to gossip. Take your quilting circle and go find someone else to hassle," he said gruffly, turning away from them.

He ignored Killian's call and walked to his car. It had been a while since he drove anywhere, and Quinn was glad he took his Range Rover today, if only so he didn't have to ride back with Killian. He had it shipped over from Portland when he moved here, but the damn thing was hard to drive in Manhattan. Still, he missed driving, something he never got to do anymore. He maneuvered it out of the garage and headed back to Lone Wolf Security.

Okay, so fine, he had been thinking about Selena the whole damn time they were in the meeting. How could he not when she was looking so fine today in that dress? The top part clung tightly to her breasts, then tapered to her small waist, and flared at the hips, the skirt ending just above her knees. He thanked several gods for the warm weather because he finally got to see Selena's shapely legs—so perfect and pale—and the image of them wrapped around his waist popped into his head.

"Motherfucker!" Quinn exclaimed as he slammed on the brakes. An old lady was crossing the street, and he had been so caught up in his fantasy that he didn't see her. The hood of his car must have stopped inches from her. The old lady glanced up at him, flashed him a dirty look, and then gave him the finger before proceeding.

Quinn banged his forehead on the wheel. He had to stop thinking about Selena that way. He had just resolved to stay away from her last night. At least he did, but his dick wasn't listening.

Clearing his head, he drove the rest of the way to Lone Wolf without any other incidents. He parked the car in the garage and went to the office. Maybe some work would help keep his mind off the redhead. *Yeah, that should help.*

As he opened the door to the office, he could smell the faint scent of butterscotch in the air. Damn. Couldn't even get any peace at work. Evie was at her desk and Luna and Meredith were sitting on the couch, but there was no sign of Selena. He nodded a greeting at both women and stalked to his office.

Quinn sat in his chair, contemplating what to do next. He thought about his conversation with Selena at the pizza shop. Was he curious about his past? Maybe. But he already knew most of the answers. His mother told him the truth, after all. Not directly, but when he grew older, he understood. The truth was Quinn was the product of an affair between his mother and her married lover.

Anna claimed to have been in love with Quinn's father, but he already had a wife and couldn't leave her. Why, he didn't know. Weren't all Lycan children cherished? Being Lycan, he should have been welcomed into his father's clan. But he wasn't. Instead, he and his mother were tossed out like garbage. Left to fend for themselves with no clan to call their own and no one to support them. When Anna died when he was ten and the authorities couldn't find any living relatives to take him in, he went into the system.

Quinn bounced around from foster home to foster home. They were all a blur to him or, at least, that's what he told himself. Any mention of the past had Wolf on edge, but still, some memories couldn't be forgotten. But he learned to survive. That was what mattered. Learned how to run away, cover his tracks. He got better each time, dodging cops and social workers who thought they were helping him by putting him back in those homes. It was only after Archie found him, huddled in some warehouse with a bunch of other delinquents, that he finally felt safe and let his guard down.

Swallowing the pain, he grabbed the handle of the bottom desk drawer and pulled it open. The envelope lay there, his name right on top. With a deep sigh, he took it and laid it on top of his desk.

*Q*uinn slumped back in the seat of his Range Rover, looking at the large house in front of him. It was a beautiful home, done in a classic Italianate style with tall arched windows and ornate decorations, low hipped roofs, and a central tower with a cupola. The brick exterior made it look warm and inviting, and he wondered if the same would be true of its occupants.

As if his life wasn't full of enough ironies, the envelope containing his past brought him to Upstate New York. Albany to be exact. Archie had been thorough in his investigation, and the

address written on the first paper inside jumped at him immediately. It was only a three-hour drive from Manhattan. Quinn
spent the whole night wondering if he should go. He didn't
sleep at all, and, finally, it was five a.m. and he was exhausted.
By the time he woke up at noon, he had decided. Curiosity had
pricked at him, and he had to find out for himself.

According to the file, Quinn's father was part of the New
York clan. He couldn't believe that his father was in the same
state. Grant Anderson probably knew him, too, though he probably wasn't Alpha yet when Quinn's mother got pregnant. Jacob
Martin. That was his name. And with a little bit of Googling,
everything clicked into place. Right around the time Quinn was
born, Jacob Martin was elected to Congress. He was one of the
youngest congressmen ever to be elected in his district. Inside
the file was a picture of his father at his victory party, standing
next to his lovely wife. With so much at stake, Martin probably
didn't want to risk news of the affair or love child being splashed
across tabloid headlines. And now, according to the billboard he
passed on the way here, Martin was running for Governor of
New York.

Quinn gripped the steering wheel. Inside him, Wolf was
going crazy. It did not like reminders of the past, and, right now,
all it wanted to do was rip something up. Archie had taught
Quinn to control the animal, and he took a deep breath, trying
to remember the lessons the old man had taught him. He really
should just walk away. He opened the envelope, confirmed what
he knew (that his biological father was a selfish, heartless
bastard), and so he didn't need to be here.

Still, Quinn couldn't scratch the itch. He opened the door of
his car and walked across the street. Now or never, he thought.
As he walked up the porch, he could feel Wolf start to get
agitated. *Get a grip.* Lycans lived in this house, and he couldn't
let them sense his damaged wolf.

He pressed the doorbell, and, by the time the door opened, he still didn't know what he was going to say. Would his father answer?

An older, attractive woman with blond hair opened the door. "Yes?"

"Um, hi." His throat closed up, and his palms suddenly got sweaty.

"Can I help you?" Her eyes narrowed into slits and her nostrils flared. Lycan. He could sense the wolf inside her. And she could sense Wolf, too.

"No. I mean, yes." *Fuck.* "I'm here to see Congressman Martin. I'm—"

"He doesn't want to see you." The woman's voice was cold and cutting.

"Excuse me?" Quinn tried to keep his voice steady and calm. Looking down at the woman, he realized who she was. She was much older now than in the picture, but she was still beautiful. His father's wife. Carla Martin. "You don't even know who I am or why I need to see him."

"I know who you are." She stepped forward and closed the door behind her. "You're that woman's son. His former secretary, Anna."

"Then you know what I am to him."

"Yes, but why you're here, I don't know." She shrugged. "Didn't your mother tell you?"

"My mother's dead."

"I'm sorry," Carla said in a voice that didn't sound sorry at all. "But she should have told you that Jacob wanted no communication from either of you."

"I just want—"

"Can't you see what you'd do to him if you keep this up?" Carla asked. "He's about to become Governor of New York. The highest office any Lycan has ever held. And, who knows, he might make it all the way to the White House. Can you imagine what that would be like? The Alpha himself has thrown his support behind Jacob. If it came out he had an affair and a son outside marriage, you wouldn't just be ruining his life but also destroying any chance our kind has to advance in politics."

"Jesus, lady," he said. "I just want to see him." He was starting to hate this bitch. No, scratch that, he already hated her.

"And then what?" Carla crossed her arms over her chest. "He doesn't want you," she added with a huff. "That should be clear by now. That's why he paid her to go away. He couldn't let the tabloids know about you and ruin his chances of getting elected."

Quinn kept his hands at his side, trying to control the turmoil of emotions running through him. His jaw tightened and his lips pursed together.

"What do you want? More money? I can give you money."

"I don't want your fucking money, lady." Quinn took a deep breath. "This was a mistake," he muttered under his breath.

"Damn right," Carla agreed. "Do us all a favor and just leave. And don't come back."

"I'm not planning to," he snarled as he turned away. His legs felt like lead, but he used all his strength to walk back to the car and get inside. As he turned the key in the ignition, he saw Carla watching him. Probably making sure he did leave. Well, rest assured, Quinn was never going to come back here again.

He stepped on the gas, following the road back to the highway. Inside him, Wolf was howling in pain, pleading with and begging him. For what? The animal whimpered. It needed comfort, soothing. He suddenly swerved onto the shoulder and then slammed his fists on the horn, letting out an anguished cry. *Goddammit.* He wished Wolf would just get angry and rip out of his skin, but the animal was too broken. Maybe because, deep down inside, he always wished that his mother was wrong. That his father did love her back and that he wanted Quinn, too. But it was evident now. Life was not a fairy tale, and there was no happy ever after in the end.

With a deep breath, he looked at the road ahead. It was a long drive, and it would be dark by the time he got to New York. *Better get a move on.*

8

_S_elena let out a satisfied moan as she sank into the warm water. There was nothing like soaking in a bubble bath at the end of the day. After lunch, she had gone back to the library and focused on work, trying to get Quinn out of her mind. The next day, she got up, went to work and kept busy until she exhausted herself. The only way to trick her brain into not thinking about Quinn was to fill it with something else.

Her conversation with the girls shook her to her very core. They all agreed Quinn was a player. Hell, she pegged him as a man-slut the moment they met. Then why couldn't she stop her heart from doing somersaults when she thought of him? Why couldn't she get his smile out of his mind? She would just have to find a way. Avoid him at all costs and forget about Quinn.

And of course, her father called again, right before she got into the bath. She told him she was still thinking about the proposal, but would make her decision soon.

The sound of the doorbell interrupted her thoughts. "Ugh. Go away," she said to no one in particular. It couldn't have been Evie. She was out late at an open mic night in East Village, and she never forgot her keys. Probably some delivery guy who was at the wrong door. Maybe, if she kept quiet, whoever it was would just go away and leave her in peace. She closed her eyes, trying to relax, but the damn doorbell kept on ringing.

"All right, all right!" She rose from the bath quickly, splashing water all over the floor. Grabbing her robe and yanking it on, she stomped to the front door, ready to give whoever was interrupting her alone time a piece of her mind. "What the fuck—Quinn?"

The Lycan was standing there, in front of her door, eerily still. His face was drawn into a scowl, and his hair was mussed up like he had been running his fingers through it.

"Wow, you look like hell," she joked, but when he didn't say anything or give a snappy comeback, she knew something was up. "Quinn? What's wrong?"

"Can I come in?" he asked in a hoarse voice. "I just ... I need to talk to someone."

The pain in his words slashed at her, and she nodded, opening the door to let him in. "Go on inside. I'll make us some tea."

Selena went to the kitchen and prepared the kettle, then opened a canister of tea, placing a bag in each mug. When the water boiled, she added it to the mugs and then went out to the living room. Quinn was sitting on the couch, his gaze straight ahead. He said nothing as she sat down and set the mugs on the coffee table.

"Quinn, tell me what's going on," she urged. "Please."

He sat there in silence for a few moments, then he spoke. "I found him. My father."

"What?" she asked. "I thought your dad was dead?"

"No," he said. "I mean, he is. Archie is gone, but I found my biological father. He's from New York."

"Quinn ... what happened?"

"I went to see him. Upstate." He paused, his hands curling into fists. "Shit. I don't know why the fuck I went there anyway. I already knew. Mom told me."

"Told you what?"

"He didn't want me," he croaked. "He never wanted me. And when I got there, I confirmed it." He buried his face in his hands.

"Quinn ..." Unsure what to do, she moved closer to him and wrapped an arm around his shoulders. "Quinn, I'm sorry. I'm so sorry." She placed her hand on his thigh, rubbing it back and forth in a soothing manner. "Look at me."

He lifted his head and turned to her, his face drawn in anguish and blue eyes stormy with emotions.

"Quinn," she continued, swallowing the lump in her throat. "That man ... whoever he is, is *not* your father. Archie was your dad, in every way that mattered. He took you in and put you back together. He gave you a home. He gave you a family."

Quinn's eyes searched hers, then glazed over. God, she didn't realize how close he was to her. She could smell his aftershave and feel the warmth of his breath. She suddenly felt conscious of how naked she was under her robe.

"Selena," he breathed, then moved his head forward to capture her mouth in a kiss.

She gasped in surprise, but she let out a moan as soon as their lips touched. Quinn's hands went up to the sides of her head to steady her. His mouth was intent on devouring her. And dear Lord, at that moment, she wanted to be devoured, to be consumed by this man until there was nothing left.

His demanding lips caressed hers, and soon Selena found herself on her back, his weight on top of her. Quinn's lips seared a path down her neck to her collarbones. As deft fingers untied the belt and parted the front of her robe, his other hand closed around her breast. She sighed when his fingers found a pink nipple and teased it.

Quinn groaned as he went lower, wrapping his lips around one of the hardened buds. He sucked on her nipple, pulling it deep into his mouth. His warm, wet mouth felt incredible, and she had never felt such a sensation before. Unsure what to do, she thrust her fingers into his hair, pulling at the locks as he continued to lave her breasts with attention.

God, all these new sensations were frying her brain. Her knees spread, and he settled himself between her legs. When the hard bulge in his pants rubbed against her core, she shivered. Quinn stiffened and then relaxed. He moved up again, staring down at her with his piercing blue eyes before leaning down to crush his lips to hers.

Selena opened up to him, their tongues dancing as they kissed. His hand moved again, down to skim over her belly and lower still. She gasped into his mouth at the first touch of his fingers over her curls and slit. He explored her expertly, fingers rubbing up and down her damp folds, then stroking her clit until she was soaking wet. Moving his hand around, two fingers slid right into her..

She cried out, her arms winding around his neck as her body moved in rhythm with his thrusting fingers. His mouth pulled away from hers but found the soft spot under her neck, and he sucked at the delicate skin. Selena bit her lip to keep from crying out, but it was useless as a sob ripped from her throat. His fingers, his lips, and the scent of grass and sawdust that threatened to overwhelm her brought her closer to orgasm. Her nails dug into his back as the wave of pleasure hit her, and she thrust her hips hard against his hand, riding it until the end.

"Selena," he rasped. "You're so beautiful when you come."

Selena gasped, her body useless and weak as she recovered from her orgasm. Quinn shifted his body and reached down between them. When she heard the unbuckling of his belt and the unzipping of his fly, a sudden fear gripped her. No, she couldn't. Her body, however, was still on fire from her orgasm and wanted more.

Quinn moaned, and she felt the tip of his cock brush against her pelvis. "Quinn ..." she pushed him gently. He looked up at her, eyes clouded with desire. "Quinn, no ..."

He stopped suddenly. "Selena?"

"I said, no!" This time, she shoved at him hard, and he nearly fell but managed to steady himself. She scrambled away from him, yanking her robe shut as she huddled on the other end of the couch. Oh God, what was she thinking? "Please," she choked. "I'm sorry. I can't ... I mean ... please leave."

"What the fuck are you saying?" Quinn's voice was edgy, almost a growl. "Selena ... I thought ..."

"You thought wrong!" she cried.

"Fucking hell I did. Or did I imagine you coming all over my fingers?"

"Shut up!" she yelled.

"C'mon, Selena," he scooted closer to her. "You can't deny it. You want me. I can smell how wet you are right now." He grabbed her hand and placed it over the hard bulge between his legs. "And I want you."

She pulled her hand away. Damn, he was right. Her body was buzzing with excitement, and she wanted to know what it would feel like to make love to Quinn. But her mind was telling her it wasn't right. "We shouldn't. You know it. This is wrong."

"Goddammit, then why is this the only thing that feels right?" With a loud growl, he jerked back and ran his hands through his hair in frustration.

"What do you want? A pity fuck?" she exclaimed. "Did you come here hoping I'd feel sorry enough to give you what you want?"

Quinn's eyes went flat and unreadable as stone, and his mouth turned into a hard line. He stood up silently and walked toward the door.

"Quinn," she called. Her stomach clenched tight, and something tore at her chest. "I—"

"I wasn't looking for a pity fuck," he said without looking back.

"Then why did you come here? What do you want?"

"I ..." he hesitated. "Never mind." He disappeared into the foyer without another word.

The sound of the door slamming seemed so final to Selena. She sat at the end of the couch, feeling like she was swimming through a haze of emotions and desire. What had they done? They almost had sex. She almost lost her virginity to Quinn. Sure, she wasn't saving it or anything, but still ... She never knew lust could be so consuming. And confusing. Selena sensed his pain, how his father's rejection was eating at him, and all she wanted to do was comfort him. But then he was kissing her and on top of her and making her feel so good ...

The sound of the door opening made her jump in surprise. Did Quinn come back?

"I'm home!" Evie announced as she barged into the apartment. "Hey Selena ..." Her best friend's expression changed as soon as it landed on her. "What's going on?"

"Evie ..." she choked.

"Selena?" Evie dropped her bag and scrambled onto the couch. "Did something happen to you?"

Tears sprang in her eyes. "Oh, Evie ..."

9

Quinn punched his fist on the keyboard and pushed at the table. The back of his chair slammed into the wall behind him. "Fucking shit!" He leaned back and closed his eyes. "Goddamn motherfucker."

Letting out a frustrated sigh, Quinn closed his eyes. Monday morning came too fast and, at the same time, it didn't come soon enough. He spent the entire weekend cooped up in his loft. His place was spacious, which was one of the reasons he bought it. Whenever he felt like shifting and couldn't get away, Wolf was usually sated by roaming around the living space and sniffing at all the interesting corners and smells. But this weekend, the animal was unmanageable. Two times, police officers had come knocking on his door when his neighbors complained about the strange noises coming from his apartment. *Goddamn nosy people.* He was glad he had enough control over Wolf to tuck him away when the cops came.

What he should have done was go out, get drunk, and find some chick he could jump into bed with and forget about Selena. But each time he made a move to leave, Wolf ripped out of him, preventing him from even opening the door. What a cock blocker. And he ripped two of his best outfits, too.

By the time Monday morning rolled around, he was edgy and on the verge of losing his goddamned mind. Thoughts of his father's rejection, then Selena's, were consuming him all weekend. What the fuck was her problem anyway? One moment she was falling apart in his arms, then the next she was shoving at him like he was the scum of the earth. She wanted his body, that was for sure. He could see it in her eyes and smell the arousal from her sweet, tight little snatch. God, all he wanted to do was bury himself in her and forget about his fucking awful day and for once, just once, feel something good and real. He thought he could have that with Selena, but he was wrong.

And now the fucking Internet wasn't working. *Fuck my life.*

"Evie," he growled as he kicked his door open. "Evie!"

"What?" she called out from the front. The irritation in her voice was evident. "I'm working."

Quinn stalked out to the reception area. "When are they going to fix the goddamn Internet? I can't get any fucking work done around here."

"I already called it in," she retorted. "Some road crew accidentally cut into a cable somewhere. They're trying to fix it now, but it'll take a while."

"Then why the hell didn't you tell me?"

"Because you've been a beast today and I didn't want to get my head bitten off," she shot back.

"What the hell is going on?" Connor suddenly appeared in the hallway, his gaze moving from Evie to Quinn. "Why the fuck are you cussing at Evie?"

Oh great, Quinn thought. Connor and his fucking weird hard-on for Evie were here. *Just what I need.* Well, if it's a fight he wants, it's a fight he's going to get. Wolf was screaming to tear something open, and he was just crazy enough to take on the feral Lone Wolf. "Stay out of this, Connor. I'll chew her out if I want to, especially if she's not doing her goddamn—" Quinn let out a choked gasp, not finishing the sentence as Connor grabbed him by the throat and slammed him back. The back of his head hit the wall so hard his brain rattled in his skull.

"You little shit," Connor growled. "You don't talk to her that way, you hear? Say you're sorry." His beefy hands were wrapped around Quinn's neck, squeezing slowly.

"Connor!" Evie cried, grabbing at his arm. "Stop, please."

Connor let go of Quinn's neck and turned to Evie. While his brother was distracted, Quinn used the opening to slam his body into Connor's, sending them both to the ground.

Evie let out a scream as they rolled on the floor, each trying to get the upper hand. Connor landed a punch in his stomach, and the air rushed out of him. The other fist got him square on the eye. Ouch. That one was going to leave a mark. Good thing for Lycan healing. While Connor was the best fighter out of all his siblings, Quinn and Wolf were determined to win. When Evie screamed Connor's name and distracted him again, Quinn used his weight against his brother, rolling on top. Quinn landed a punch on Connor's jaw, but his brother merely grunted in response, then slammed his fist into Quinn's side. Pain shot through him, but he held steady, digging his knees into either side of Connor.

"Stop!" Killian's voice boomed through the reception area. "What the fuck is going on here? Quinn, get off Connor before you get yourself killed."

"Me?" Quinn growled as he got to his feet, blood dripping down over his eye and onto the carpet. "I had him!"

"You and I both know Connor could rip you apart, even on a bad day," Killian said. "Now, what is going on?"

Connor got up, pulling himself to full height and puffing out his chest. "This fucking idiot was rude to Evie for no goddamn reason other than he's been having a shitty day. He screamed at her."

"Is this true?" Killian asked Quinn. "Were you rude to her?"

Quinn let out a huff. Damn, what could he say? "Yes." He turned to Evie. "I'm sorry."

Evie was on the verge of tears with her hands wringing together. "I don't forgive you. You're such an asshole." She walked over to her desk and grabbed her purse. "I need to go." She looked at Killian. "I have that ... other thing I told you about, Boss."

"I understand," Killian said. "Go ahead."

Evie gave him a curt nod and headed toward the door.

Shit. "Evie, no, please."

Quinn tried to make a grab for her arm, but she evaded him. "You said you wouldn't hurt her and you did!" Evie's chin trembled as she spoke. "She's a virgin, you dick. She was scared, and she didn't know how to tell you!" With that, she pivoted and left the office, the door slamming behind her.

Quinn remained rooted to the spot, his mouth hanging open. *Selena's a virgin?* Goddamn. Now he really was scum.

"What the fuck is going on?" Killian yelled at Quinn. "Why were you guys fighting and who's a virgin? Did you try to fuck Evie?"

"What?" Quinn asked. The air suddenly grew dense and a loud growl from behind suddenly made him want to cower in fear. *Goddamn Connor.* "Fuck, no, not Evie! Selena!"

"Wait, you tried to sleep with Selena? Evie's friend?"

"Yeah ... Um, it's a long story."

Killian and Connor stared at him as if waiting for an explanation. He rolled his eyes. "Goddammit, are we going to start drinking wine while we talk about our feelings? Fuck you guys. I'm outta here."

Quinn stalked to the door, yanked it open, and stepped out, making sure to slam it behind him as loud as he could. He stormed to the elevator, jabbing his finger at the call button.

"Fuck!" he cursed aloud. Selena ... no wonder she was scared. She was comforting him, being a good friend, and then what did he do? Try to fuck her the first chance he got. Shit. He was a lowlife, that's what he was. Wolf growled in agreement. *Yeah, buddy, tell me about it.* But what was he supposed to do now? Selena probably wouldn't want to talk to him. But he had to see her, make sure she was okay, and apologize. Again. Dammit, he couldn't seem to do anything but hurt her. After this, he was going to stay away from her. For real this time and for good. But that ache inside him wouldn't go away until he at least said his peace.

10

*Q*uinn wasn't surprised at all that Selena wasn't at work. He probably traumatized her. Shit, he didn't want to say it, but he was all over her and if she didn't say no ... Fuck.

The fact that Selena was a virgin still blew his mind. How could anyone that gorgeous stay untouched? Surely some guy would have snapped her up by now. Thinking about her with some guy made his chest ache. But no, if she was a virgin ...

"Goddammit." Talk about an inappropriate time to have an erection. He quickly walked away before some parent or cop saw him sporting a chubby right outside a public library. Still, the thought of Selena untouched made something primal in him rise up, and he wasn't just talking about his dick. He was probably the first man to touch her pussy and make her moan like that. Dammit, thinking about her delicious, untouched body and her soft tits wasn't making this any better. He didn't just need a cold shower; he needed a dunking in the polar ice caps.

He hailed a cab and gave the driver Selena's address. It was a long trip, and, unfortunately, a wasted one. As he stood outside her front door, his keen hearing couldn't pick up any sounds coming from the inside. Where the hell was she? He never thought to get her number.

He fished his phone out of his pocket and tried to call Evie, but her phone was off. There was only one person who knew where Selena could be and that was Evie. But there was only one person who knew where Evie was, and he hoped he hadn't pissed off Killian too much.

"Hello?" Killian answered when Quinn called his number.

"Kill, it's me," he said.

"Where the hell are you?"

"I need to know where Evie is," Quinn said. "You know where she is, don't you?"

Killian let out an exasperated sigh. "Don't make things worse with her, you hear?"

"I won't. Selena's gone. I mean, I don't know where she is, and Evie turned her phone off."

"All right, I'll tell you, but don't tell anyone else. She told me as a courtesy, but asked I keep it to myself."

"Why the hell are you whispering?" Quinn asked in an irritated voice.

"Because Connor is in his office and he might hear what I'm about to tell you."

"Right." He paused. "Well?"

Killian's muffled voice came through the receiver, saying the name of a place they were all familiar with.

"Goddamn," Quinn laughed. "You're right to worry about Connor. What is she doing there?"

"How the hell should I know? I'm not her secretary. Just go and say you're sorry. You better make things right with her or I swear, if she quits, I'm going to make you and Connor organize the file cabinets and order supplies for the office."

Quinn shuddered, though the image of Connor labeling folders and working with spreadsheets filled him with glee. "I will. I promise."

---

*Q*uinn stood outside the nondescript warehouse in Soho, hands on his hips, and stared at the massive metal door. To most people, it probably looked like any other converted factory building in Manhattan, but only a few knew the secrets behind the brick walls and darkly-tinted windows.

Merlin's was a secret witch club in New York. A male strip club that catered to the magical community to be exact. When he and his siblings were investigating Archie's death, they discovered Merlin's was the last place he was before he was murdered. They had to go undercover to find out what their father was doing in such a place and Quinn, of course, volunteered to work as an 'entertainer,' along with Daric. While he didn't take the stage, he had a chance to entertain some very uninhibited and lively witches at a private party. Of course, that evening didn't exactly turn out as he'd expected (which was, aside from finding out who murdered Archie, score with a witch or two), seeing as Wolf decided to make an appearance when their witness, Sven, tried to run away. After being hit with a strong confounding potion that gave him a headache for hours, it was understandable why he didn't want to step foot in Merlin's again.

But what the fuck was Evie doing here?

He walked closer, examining the door. Tuning his sharp ears, he could hear noises and music coming from inside. Unfortunately, the din made it hard to figure out if Evie was in there.

The first time they were here, they were thinking of ways to break in to find out what was inside. Daric (though formerly evil, wasn't a criminal like them) was the only one who thought to knock. Hmmm ... maybe that would work too.

Quinn raised his fist and rapped his knuckles on the door. He waited, and then moments later, the door slid open.

"You again," the squat, balding man said with an annoyed snort. "Did you come back for more potion, Lycan?"

"No thanks, last time was plenty."

"Then what do you want?" Ivar said, his piercing green eyes narrowing at him.

"I'm looking for someone. Evie. King."

He frowned. "Ms. King is indisposed."

"Well, I'm going to in-dispose of your ass if you don't let me in."

"Why you—"

"Ivar?" A smooth voice called from behind the door. "Who's there?" Lucien Merlin's head popped out from behind Ivar. "Oh, it's you. Quinn, right? What are you doing here? Looking to make some extra cash? I might have an opening for the two a.m. slot on Wednesdays."

"Jesus, no." Quinn slapped a hand over his forehead. "I'm looking for Evie."

"Evie?" The handsome warlock frowned. "Oh, you mean Guinevere," he said, mentioning Evie's full name. "She's here, but she's working."

"I have to see her."

Merlin crossed his arms over his chest, and his inky black eyes seemed to pierce right into him. "Really? What for?"

"I ..." Shit. He wanted to make an emergency at Lone Wolf, but something about Merlin made him think twice about lying. So he decided to go for the truth. "I'm here because I was rude to her and I want to say sorry. And make sure she's okay." Part of the truth anyway.

"Ah, so that's why she seemed a little snippy today." Merlin let out an exasperated sigh. "I suppose you can come in, but if she doesn't want to speak with you, then you're going to have to leave."

"Fine."

Merlin crooked a finger at him. "Follow me, handsome."

Ivar slid the door open to let him in, and Quinn followed the warlock into the main room of Merlin's. It was just as he remembered—red carpets, red walls, red lights. It was a classy joint but definitely screamed of sex.

"I made a few changes," Merlin said as they walked towards the stage. "To our lineup and our entertainment. First, despite your little show on that night, you were a big hit with my regular clientele, so I found a couple of shifters who were looking for a good way to earn money."

"No shit, huh?" Quinn laughed. "Turning into a wolf in front of a room full of witches and warlocks was good for business after all. Maybe I deserve a cut?"

Merlin smirked. "I'm still paying for the damage you caused, by the way. Do you think I use cheap glass here? No, crystal only, including the chandeliers you broke. Anyway, here you go."

Quinn swerved his head toward the main stage. There were about a dozen male dancers wearing nothing but black underwear and knee-high leather boots. In the center was Evie, talking to another well-built man who was just as naked as the others, save for a sparkly red jacket and top hat. Evie was holding a riding crop and was showing sparkly jacket how to smack it against one of the dancer's buttocks.

Holy shit. Quinn had a great idea. He whipped out his phone and snapped a picture of Evie the exact moment the crop hit the guy's ass.

"Hey, hey, no pictures," Merlin warned. "We haven't debuted our new show yet."

"What the fuck is going on here?" Quinn asked, gesturing to the stage. "You turning this place into an S & M dungeon now?"

"I told you," Merlin drawled. "I'm making a few changes. One of them being the entertainment."

"All right, guys," Evie called. "Let's take it from the top! Jack," she said to sparkly jacket man. "Good job, keep it up, okay?"

"Thanks, babe," he said, flashing her a smile that was full of pearly white teeth.

Evie turned to walk down the steps from the stage to the main floor, and as she neared the bottom, her eyes landed on Quinn. "Quinn! What are you doing?"

"I'm texting Connor," he said matter-of-factly, attaching the photo to his message. This was payback for the black eye and bruised rib.

"I mean, what are you doing *here*? And what do you mean you're texting Connor?"

"Haha," Quinn cackled as he opened his contacts folder. "Connor's gonna get a big surprise in his inbox in 3 … 2 …"

"Quinn!" Evie lunged at him, but Quinn was too tall and too quick. He pulled the phone out of her reach and pressed send.

"What the hell do you think you're doing?"

"Just getting back at my brother for this," he said, pointing to his eye.

"You big baby, it's already healing. It'll be gone in a few hours. Now," she put her hands on her hips. "What did you say to Connor?"

"Nothing!" When Evie gave him the stink-eye, he relented. "I just sent him a nice picture of you doing your best dominatrix impression."

"Quinn!" she screamed. "You idiot! I was showing Jack how to do it for the show! I'm directing a segment for Merlin's new lineup!"

"Huh?" He looked up at the stage as the music began to play and the dancers moved around Jack. It was like he was playing a ringmaster and the dancers around him were circus animals. With the staging, costumes, and music (that guy sure could sing), the show was tasteful. Very Broadway, with less clothing.

"Uh, you're such an asshole," Evie pouted. "How could you text him that?"

"Why would it matter to you, anyway?" he asked. "Do you have anything to hide? Is that why you told Killian about working here but not me and Connor?"

"You don't understand."

He cocked his head. "Tell me, do you have a crush on Connor?"

"What?" Evie turned red. "No! I do not."

"Because you know, only women with a special kind of crazy go after Connor." Quinn raised a brow at her. "Are you that special kind of crazy, Evie? Maybe if you do fuck him, he'll finally relax."

Evie bit her lip. "How did you get in here? And what do you want?"

"I've been here before," he said. "And well ... kidding aside, I came here to say sorry to you and to ask you if you've seen ... Selena?"

A flash of auburn hair from the corner of his eye made Quinn whip his head to the right of the stage. There she was. Selena, waiting in the wings, talking to some guy. A guy dressed in nothing but a black speedo and a smile.

"What the fuck is she doing here?" he growled. Wolf was gnashing its teeth, screaming at him to go there and wipe that smile off the man's face.

"She got me this job. Of course, she's here, she's—"

Quinn's vision went red, and he didn't hear the rest of Evie's sentence. He marched up the steps, much to the annoyance of the performers on stage, and headed straight to Selena and her beefcake.

11

*S*elena laughed as Brad told her the story of how he met one of their teachers on some hook up app. She hadn't seen him in years, not since they went to high school together; she didn't even know that he worked at Merlin's. Brad said he enjoyed the job and being around other warlocks. She understood, as she missed life with the coven, the sense of community and feeling safe. She probably would visit more often if it weren't for her stepsisters.

"Oh my God, Brad!" She swatted him playfully on the shoulder. "No. Way. Mr. Jenkins?"

"Oh yes way, Selena," he laughed. "His profile said he was a papa bear looking for his baby bear."

"I don't even know what that means ... so what happened?"

"Well, we went to the backseat of his car and—"

"Selena."

The familiar voice made her freeze. *It couldn't be.* Slowly, she pivoted toward the speaker. "Quinn?"

Quinn's mouth was pulled into a hard line, and his jaw was set tight. "What are you doing here?"

Selena's expression went quickly from surprise to irritation.

"Excuse me, what am *I* doing here? What about you? What are *you* doing here?"

"I came here to say sorry to Evie," he answered in a clipped voice. "Wow, you sure do recover quickly," he said, his eyes flickering to Brad.

"Who is this guy and what the fuck is he talking about, Sel?" Brad asked.

Irritation was now going to full-blown anger, and Selena felt the pressure building behind her eyes. "You jerk. What gives you the right to come here and judge me?"

"Well, it's true, right? What, you can't stand a Lycan touching you, but you'll gladly fool around with some warlock stripper?"

"Entertainer," Brad interjected. "We're changing our job titles to entertainer now."

"For your information," Selena retorted, putting her hands on her hips. "Brad is a friend from high school. I ran into him, and I didn't know he worked here."

"And just what are you doing here, anyway?"

"I got Evie this job. I recommended her to Uncle Lucien."

Quinn's eyes bulged from their sockets. "Uncle?"

"Yeah, you jackass," Brad said in an annoyed voice. "Her last name should have given you a clue. Selena Merlin."

"Wait," Quinn turned to Selena. "Merlin is your last name?"

"Yes!" she yelled at him. She couldn't believe she was having this conversation with Quinn. And that he was even here. "Ugh! I can't do this." She threw her hands up in the air and pivoted, walking away from Quinn and Brad. She wasn't sure where she was going, but anywhere far away from Quinn sounded like a good idea right now.

After Quinn had left that night and she poured her heart out to Evie, they decided to get drunk—very drunk—consuming every drop of alcohol in the apartment. And then, three sheets to the wind, they thought it would be a good idea to go out and find more booze, but seeing as neither had the extra funds to go out drinking at expensive clubs and bars, Selena suggested they go to Merlin's. After all, even though their first and last outing to the club hadn't gone too well, her Uncle Lucien had told her they were welcome anytime.

So, they took an Uber downtown to Merlin's. Uncle Lucien (who was not Selena's father's brother but more like a distant cousin) had welcomed them into his private booth and gave them more (free) alcohol. Selena refused to talk about why she was trying to drown her sorrows, but Evie, who was coming home from another failed audition, went on and on about how she was never going to get on a Broadway stage and that she'd never get to exercise her creative side. That was when Uncle Lucien was struck with inspiration—why not come work for him and help him revamp Merlin's? The warlock had been trying to come up with ideas to drum up new business, and he thought that creating a sensual cabaret (as opposed to his usual male strip show) might help. Evie immediately jumped at the chance and so, come Monday (after they spent Sunday recovering from the hangovers), they both arrived at Merlin's. Evie worked on a couple of ideas with the dancers and Selena took the day off to support her friend.

And, now, Quinn had somehow found them. Damn him. She was determined to forget him and try to move on. But then, all he had to do was show his handsome face, and she was a goner. Even though he was a jerk to Brad, her mind kept replaying that night in her apartment and how Quinn tasted and how his fingers felt so good inside her. No man had ever touched her down there. She felt the warmth creep up her neck. God, she had to get out of here before she embarrassed herself.

She walked down the hallway behind the stage, deciding that she would circle back and go to the left side of the stage, then maybe try and slip out the back before anyone noticed she was gone.

"Selena! Selena, stop!" Quinn's voice rang down the narrow passageway.

"Get away from me!" She picked up her pace, but it was no use. Quinn's long strides made up for her head start and he caught her arm, whipping her around to face him.

"Selena, please, I'm sorry," he said.

"Take your hands off me," she cried. "I don't want to see you."

"Selena, you gotta listen to me, please." He pulled her up against the wall, his hands on either side of her so she couldn't escape. "I know that you've never been with anyone before. Evie told me."

Selena's cheeks went hot as if someone poured gasoline on them and struck a match. "She shouldn't have said anything."

"No, I'm glad she did." When she turned away, unable to meet his gaze, he touched a finger to her chin and tipped her face up to meet his bright blue gaze, almost glowing in the low light of the backstage. "I'm sorry for what I said. I was out of line, and I was frustrated. I shouldn't have taken it out on you. But I'm not sorry for what we did. Selena, I wanted you so bad. I still want you now. You're beautiful and sexy, and I just couldn't help myself."

Selena stared up at him, trying to process his words. Quinn thought she was beautiful and wanted her? Still? "Quinn ..." She reached up and placed a hand on his jaw, running up to his stubbly cheek, the rough hair tickling her fingers.

All her life, Selena had done nothing but give while the people around her did nothing but take. When her mom died, she was the one who took care of her father, even though she was only twelve years old. When Leonard decided to get remarried two years later, she swallowed the bitterness and pretended to be happy for him, even when Alexis and Katrina's cruel treatment made her cry herself to sleep. When her sisters took her things, her friends, and her boyfriends, she accepted it to keep peace in the family. And now, just for tonight, she wanted this one thing. To be selfish, just for a moment.

"Quinn," she breathed. "I want you, too. Let's go back to your place."

His pupils blew up with desire. "Selena ... are you sure?"

"Yes, I'm sure," she said with a nod. "Take me away, please."

---

*A*s soon as the words left Selena's mouth, Quinn sprang into action. He whisked her away from Merlin's and hailed a cab, giving the driver his address in a hurried voice. It was like he was afraid she would change her mind again and wanted to make damn sure she didn't this time. They soon arrived at his loft, and Quinn wasted no time getting them through the door.

"Wait," she said, putting a hand on his chest as he approached her.

Did she change her mind already? He let out a sigh. He respected her, of course, and would never even think of making her do anything she didn't want. "What is it? Do you want to go home?"

"No," she said with a shake of her head. "I just want to make something clear." She took a deep breath. "About what you said before. I understand, and I agree."

"Huh?" What the fuck was she talking about?

"I just want you to know that I remember what you said about not wanting a relationship and I respect that. I'm not going to trap you into anything. After tonight, you're free to do whatever you want."

He ignored the pang in his heart at her words. "Of course. We're in agreement. Now," he backed her up against the wall. "Are you ready?"

"Yes."

He swooped his head down, bringing their lips together in a searing kiss that sent his nerve endings on fire. Damn, she tasted sweet, and it was like he was drunk. Drunk on Selena and her mouth and her butterscotch scent. He grabbed her thighs, lifted her up against the wall, and then pushed his hips to hers so she could feel how much he wanted her. She let out a whimper and wrapped her legs around his waist, grinding her heated core against him.

Quinn held onto her tighter, his hands going around her, and walked them to his bedroom. He strode over to his bed, laying her down gently. He felt like he was in a dream, seeing Selena on the sheets, her wild red mane loose and flowing over the pillows. God, she was gorgeous as she looked up at him, desire glittering in her blue-gray eyes. She watched him undress down to his underwear, her gaze flickering briefly to the wolf's head tattoo on the right side of his chest. He shucked off his pants and kneeled on the bed.

"I ... I don't know ... what should I do?"

"Just do what feels right," he said, crawling over her. He unbuttoned her blouse, one at a time like he was unwrapping a precious gift. He parted the fabric, revealing her perfect breasts encased in white lace.

"Selena ..." he groaned, feeling more blood rush into his dick. He couldn't remember being harder than he was now.

A blush crept up her neck and her cheeks as his hands cupped her breasts. They were so fucking gorgeous and fit his large hands perfectly. His fingers traced up, yanking the straps and cups down to free her tits. The pale pink nipples hardened, and he leaned down to take one in his mouth.

"Quinn!" she cried, her hands digging into his hair, and he moaned when her fingernails scratched his scalp.

He teased her nipples with his tongue and teeth, pressing her tits together so he could suck on both at the same time.

"Oh, please, Quinn!"

He loved hearing his name on her lips, especially when she was moaning in pleasure. With a sigh, he released her nipples, though he really could have feasted on them the whole night. But there was something else he'd wanted to taste for a while now.

"Shhh ... kitten," he mouthed against her skin as he moved lower. He tugged at her pants, unhooking the clasp and then pulling them down. White lace panties that matched the bra covered her hips, the shadow of her dark red curls barely visible. He pulled those off too, revealing her sex, already wet with wanting. "I wonder if you taste as good as you smell?"

"Quinn!"

The first touch of his tongue on her pussy sent her hips bucking up against him. He steadied her, pushing her down on the bed. She squirmed underneath him but remained steady. Pressing his lips against her wet cunt, he tasted her, lapping up her juices and caressing her with his mouth. He positioned his hand over her mound, finding her clit and stroking it with his thumb. She was sweet, too sweet, and he rubbed his hard cock on the mattress, the friction giving him some relief.

She screamed his name, and her soft thighs clamped around his head as her hips pushed up off the bed, her body shaking as an orgasm raced through her body. Selena let out a whimper as her hips crashed down, and he caught her, digging his fingers into her ass. Quinn licked a stripe up her slit before sitting up on his heels. He reached over to the side and opened his side table drawer, pulling out a foil wrapper. He tried to steady his hands as he pulled his underwear off, tore the packet open with his teeth, and rolled the condom over his cock.

"Tell me if it's too much," he said. Her eyes were wide as she looked at his cock, a glint of fear in her eyes. "Don't worry, it won't bite."

"I hope not," she giggled, her body relaxing.

Quinn positioned himself between her legs, spreading her thighs apart. He braced himself on one elbow, and he reached down. She was still wet. *Good.* He slipped a finger in her and her muscles clenched. Slowly, he inserted another, and then another. God, she was so tight. He tried to stretch her with his fingers, thrusting in gently.

Her hands clutched at his forearms. "Please, Quinn ... no more teasing."

He let out a breath. "I don't want to hurt you."

"You won't," she answered, her eyes full of resolve. "Just ... I need you. Inside me. Now."

Her words made him growl, and he withdrew his fingers from her. He positioned the tip of his cock at her entrance, pushing in slowly. Selena gasped, then bit her lip when he stopped. He felt Selena's tightness around him and her back going stiff. He had to take a deep breath to calm down.

"Selena," he murmured and bent his head down low until their lips were barely touching. "I'm sorry."

His mouth muffled her cry when he pushed into her, breaking through the barrier. Selena clung to him, digging her nails down his back, but he ignored the pain. Slipping his hands underneath her, he cradled her, whispering soothing words into her ear until her body relaxed.

"Are you okay?"

She nodded against his shoulder. "I'm fine," she sighed.

"Tell me to stop if it hurts."

"I will."

Quinn gritted his teeth and braced himself. He stared down at her beautiful face, her soft pink lips, and her peach-tinted skin with a smattering of light freckles across the bridge of her nose. Her lids were shut, and her sweeping lashes cast shadows across her cheeks. "Selena," he breathed, and her eyes flew open. Brilliant blue-gray orbs fixed on him, unblinking. "Selena," he repeated as he moved his hips. One, two, three small thrusts, just to gauge her reaction. A breath escaped her mouth, and she moved her hands down, over his lower back, lightly scraping at his skin.

Encouraged by her reaction, he moved more. She was so tight and hot; he was afraid he'd blow his load right then and there, so he did it slowly. He pulled his hips back, easing out of her halfway, and then thrust back in. Selena moaned, her eyes rolling back, and a small whimper of pleasure escaped her mouth. Sweat formed on his brow as he controlled the urge to just fuck into her harder, but he had to get a hold of himself. This was Selena, not some girl he picked up from some bar or Tinder for a quick lay.

"Quinn, more," she demanded. Her fingers dug into his ass, urging him deeper. "I need more."

He snarled, the sound ripping from his throat as he picked up his pace, swinging his hips, going gentler when he saw her wince. Soon, she was moaning and sighing, little gasps that made him want to please her more. Reaching down between them, he plucked at her clit as he slid in and out her. Fuck, she felt so good, wrapped around him, his cock dragging along her tight passage. Selena was gasping again, and he leaned down to kiss her, sliding his tongue along hers.

He was really moving now. Though she was still tightly grasped around him, it was getting easier to sink into her. His hips pummeled, faster and faster into her, filling her to the hilt with his cock. He was hanging on by a thread, so he gave her clit a hard pinch, which made her throw back her head and cry out his name. Her pussy gripped him tight, squeezing so hard around him he had to slow down. Her body thrashed underneath his, and her fingers clutched at his hair as her orgasm crashed through her.

Quinn gave one last savage thrust as he lost control, spilling his seed as his orgasm hit him, sending him shuddering with pleasure. "Fuck," he cried out, grabbing her hips as he pushed deep inside, his heart hammering in his chest, the tremors refusing to stop. He crashed on top of her, though her small squeal of protest made him prop himself up to prevent his weight from crushing her.

He laid his head on her breasts, listening as the thundering beat of her heart began to slow down. With a small grunt, he eased out of her and rolled to his side, facing away from her. Discreetly, he pulled the condom off and tied off the end, chucking it into the trash bin beside the bed. He rolled over, expecting Selena's warm body next to his, but all he got was empty air.

"Selena?" He looked up.

She was standing by the bed, still naked. Her head turned, and she smiled as she stood there, wild red curls all over her shoulders and down her back, her skin still flushed from pleasure.

"Hey," she said shyly. "Have you seen my panties?"

He sat up and looked around. A scrap of lace was wedged under his leg. Snatching it, he offered it to her. "Here."

She turned around and leaned over, making a grab for the underwear. As soon as she was within reach, he wrapped his fingers around her wrist and pulled her back onto the bed.

"Quinn!" she protested as her body slid along his and she lay on top of him.

He nuzzled at her neck, giving her a playful nip. "Where do

you think you're going?" He slid his hand down her back, scraping lightly at the soft skin

She whimpered at his touch. "I ... was ... going ... home."

Quinn rolled her over, pinning her to the mattress. "It's only eight o'clock, kitten," he said with a nod to the clock on his bedside.

"But—"

He stopped her protest with a kiss. "I thought you said you wanted one night? The night's not over." He covered her mouth again before she could object. She wanted one night with him? Well, he'd give her that then. The whole night. He would have her and fuck her senseless until they both had their fill.

"Quinn ..."

"Hmmm?"

"Quinn ... stop ..."

Quinn looked up from between her legs, an annoyed look on his face. "You seriously want me to stop *now*?"

"No, but ..." Selena cocked her head to the clock on the bedside table. The red numbers on the face read 12:01.

"Isn't it daylight savings time or something?" he said "I don't think I changed the time on that thing."

"Right. Wait a minute, it's spring so ... ohhh!"

"Quinn ..."

He stopped in mid-thrust. "What now?"

"My Uber's almost here," she said.

"When the hell did you have time to book an Uber?"

"You were snoozing for a bit," she said. "And so I booked one in advance."

"Cancel it," he growled.

"But it's three a.m."

Quinn grabbed a pillow and tossed it at the clock, knocking it off the side table. "It's still dark out. That still counts as tonight."

"Quinn!"

---

*B*y the time morning came, all excuses were gone. Frankly, Quinn was too exhausted to protest when she rolled out of bed after another round. Despite her eagerness to leave, Selena was insatiable. Not that he minded. He thought he'd get enough after the first time, but each taste of her made him want more. The gnawing at his chest grew as he watched her walk into the bathroom, her clothes in hand.

He rolled onto his back and placing his arm over his eyes to block out the goddamned rays of light filtering in through the windows. This was what he wanted, right? No clinging, no attachments. Waking up next to her was already breaking the rules. He never waited for morning to leave, much less had anyone stay over.

When he heard the shower turn on, he imagined her full breasts slick with water and suds. He groaned, and it took every ounce of his will power not to go in there and screw her silly against the tiles.

He got out of bed, slipped his jeans on, and walked down the steps from his lofted bedroom to the main living area. Padding over to the kitchen, he decided to make breakfast. Their last meal was hours ago, leftover Chinese food, which they ate right after he bent her over the kitchen island and pounded into her as she gripped the edge of the granite top. Kitchen sex was going to be up there on his list of must-dos from now on.

He busied himself making eggs, toast, and coffee, humming as he prepared two plates of food.

"Smells wonderful. I didn't know you cooked."

Quinn turned his head. Selena was standing there, dressed in her clothes from the night before, leaning against the island. "Did you think I survived on Chinese takeout and cereal?" he joked. Taking the two plates, he placed one in front of her. "Eat."

"I have to run. I have to be at work in 45 minutes."

"C'mon, you have time for a bite," he coaxed. "You're, what, ten minutes away from work by cab?"

"Fine," she relented, taking a mouthful of eggs. "Hmmm, this is good."

Quinn tried not to stare as her tongue darted out to lick her pink mouth. "So," he cleared his throat. "I ... uh ... what ..." Fucking hell. He was like some teenager with his first crush.

Selena put her fork down with a loud clatter. "You're not going to make this weird are you Quinn?"

"What?" he asked, his voice pitching higher than he wanted. "No. I mean," he let out a huff and crossed his arms over his chest, "no weirdness. At all."

"Good," she said in a resolute voice. She walked around the island and closed the distance between them. "It was fun."

"Yeah ..." He stared down at her, so close he could smell her intoxicating butterscotch scent.

"And so, thanks. For everything." She got on her tiptoes, and he leaned down, expecting a kiss, but she only brushed her lips on his cheek. "I had a good time," she whispered, before stepping away.

"Yeah, sure. I mean, me too."

With one last smile, she turned around and walked to the

door. Quinn watched her pick up her purse from the console table and then open the door. When the lock clicked into place, he jolted out of his trance but was still unable to move.

At that moment, he thought of that old saying: *Be careful what you wish for; it just might come true.*

12

"Quinn? Quinn, did you hear me?"

"Huh?" Quinn started, nearly jumping out of the chair in front of Killian's desk. His brother gave him a strange look, then shook his head.

"Fucking space cadet," Connor muttered.

"Hey Connor," Quinn began. "I tried calling you last night. What happened to your phone?"

Connor let out a growl, and his fingers gripped on the arms of the chair so hard, the metal bent.

"I tracked it, you know," Quinn continued with a smile. "Looks like someone threw it in the East River."

"Quinn," Killian warned. "Stop."

"So, what were you saying again?" Quinn asked.

"Get the fuck out of here, both of you," he ordered. "Neither of you is going to get work done today. We'll come back tomorrow."

Connor stood up, his chair making a loud scraping sound as the legs dragged on the floor. He spun around and walked out the door, slamming it behind him with a loud crash.

"What the hell did you do this time?" Killian asked.

"What me?" he said, giving his brother an innocent look.

"I swear to God, someday ..." Killian grabbed his jacket. "I'm heading home. You want a ride or did you drive today?"

"Nah, I'm good." Quinn rose from his chair. "See ya tomorrow, Kill."

Quinn helped Killian close up the office, then made his way out of the building. It was a beautiful spring day, after all, and being cooped up in the office wasn't good for him or Wolf. The animal was being a whiny little bitch for the past two days. At least he made it out of the apartment last night, though still no action. He decided to avoid Blood Moon since Wolf was on edge. The problem was the damn thing kept trying to escape from his skin whenever he even got near another girl at the club.

It had been two days since Selena left his loft, and he hadn't heard from her since. He supposed he could have picked up the phone, but that wasn't his style. Usually, it was the girls who called him up, though he realized they still hadn't exchanged numbers.

Not that he needed or wanted it now. They were both adults, both knew what they wanted and didn't want. And what he didn't want was to have some chick smothering him and cramping his style. At least, that's what he told himself. Still, the memory of Selena's naked body underneath him was hard to erase. He was going to get fucking carpal tunnel syndrome if he didn't stop jerking off about five times a day to thoughts of Selena's luscious body. He just needed to get laid again. Yeah, that was it.

"Motherfucker."

Quinn was standing outside the Lower Manhattan Library. He looked up at the sign, just to make sure he wasn't dreaming. How the hell did he walk over here? *Shit.* He pivoted on his heels. He had to get out of here before—

"Quinn?"

Fuck. The mere sound of her voice had him sporting a half-chubby. He plastered on a casual smile. "Selena," he greeted, turning around. There she was, standing just outside the doors, looking so innocently sexy in a tight, pencil-cut skirt and a prim blouse buttoned up to her neck. She left her hair in wild curls around her shoulders, and he had a vision of her in bed, her hair spread over his pillows. Forget half chub; he was going full salute at this point.

Her face was drawn into a deep frown. "What are you doing here?"

"What, did you get the library in the divorce or something?" he said. "Last I checked, this was a public building."

"Fine," she said in a chilly voice, then walked past him.

"Hey, c'mon now." He seized her arm. "Don't be like that."

"I thought you said you weren't going to make this weird," she accused.

He rolled his eyes. "I'm not. I swear, scout's honor," he said, putting his hand over his heart.

"That's the Pledge of Allegiance," she pointed out.

"I wasn't a boy scout."

"I didn't think so," she said, a slight smile tugging at her lips.

Ha! He knew he had her now. "So, I was thinking—"

"Don't wear yourself out."

"Oh, haha, funny," he smirked. "I haven't finished the *Lord of the Rings* movies yet. You know, Rohan was my favorite part of the whole series."

"I'm sure you can order the Blu-Rays," she said.

"I thought we should finish what we started." Before she could protest, he continued. "The trilogy, I mean."

"Quinn," she said in a low voice. "I don't think that's a good idea." Selena pinched her lips together. "We shouldn't hang out anymore. Not alone, anyway."

"Why not?" he challenged.

She made an impatient sound. "You know why."

Quinn crossed his arms over his chest. "No, tell me. Why can't two friends hang out and watch movies together." Feeling bold, he leaned forward and whispered in her ear. "Are you afraid you're going to jump me? Didn't get enough of the Quinn experience? It's okay, I understand." He shrugged. "If you don't trust yourself, then maybe you're right. I wouldn't want you to take advantage of me."

"Fine," she snapped. "Let's go. But you're paying for the pizza and beer."

I must be out of my mind, Selena thought as they sat on the couch finishing the large Hawaiian pizza. But when it came to Quinn, she wasn't surprised. One moment, he infuriated her and the next, he was so sweet. Without having to ask, he ordered her favorite pizza, then carefully picked off the pineapples on his slices.

Then there was the fact that she couldn't stop thinking about him and his body. Quinn in his tight shirt and holey jeans was hot, but naked ... dear Lord, talk about panties on fire. Just thinking about his broad shoulders, that wolf's head tattoo covering the right part of his chest, those perfectly-formed pecs, and that defined six pack made her mouth water. She could feast on his body all day and never feel hungry.

The ache between her legs wouldn't go away, no matter how many times she touched herself. Evie probably thought she had turned into a germaphobe, taking so many baths in two days. Quinn had turned her into a sex addict. She wondered if it would go away if she got married to Jason.

Selena let out a heavy sigh. For some reason, she couldn't

muster up any guilt over what she had done. She thought it would eat away at her, but instead, she felt ... nothing. She was still dodging her father's calls and hoping to put off making the decision as long as she possibly could. If she did decide to marry Jason, then that would mean she could move back to her coven, enjoy the status of being his wife and mother to their children, and maybe Alexis and Katrina would get off her back. The prospect was tempting, but the thought of what she had to do to get that was making the hollow in her stomach grow.

"Ready for the movie?" Quinn asked as he polished off the last piece of pizza.

"Sure," she said, getting up from the couch. The smell of his aftershave was tickling her nose and sent spirals of heat through her, so the distance was a relief. She popped in the disc and sat on the other end of the couch, as far away from him as possible.

Selena played the movie and relaxed her body, trying to appear casual. Glancing over at Quinn, she pouted at how indifferent he seemed, despite their proximity. His attention was fixed on the movie, while her little whore of a body was screaming for him. Hmmm, he was probably used to it. He probably slept with so many girls that it didn't even bother him anymore. Jealousy stabbed right through her gut, and she bit her lip, trying not to let it bother her.

"Stop looking at me like that," he muttered, his eyes never leaving the screen.

She meant to say, "Like what?" in a casual voice, but instead, when she opened her mouth, a soft whimper came out.

Quinn was on her so fast her head started spinning. His lips smashed against hers, and his kisses were desperate and rough as their tongues and teeth clashed. She opened up to him, spreading her legs to accommodate him between them. His erection was grinding up against her through her panties, and she let out a moan as friction sent shivers through her. Out of curiosity, last night she had Googled "*average penis size*," and when she saw the answer, her eyes went as wide as saucers. Quinn was definitely *not* average.

"Selena," he mouthed against her neck.

God, they shouldn't. No, they couldn't. Yet, she didn't protest when Quinn's hand went right under her skirt, touching her already damp pussy. She purred in pleasure as his fingers slipped inside her, thrusting into her as she ground her hips up against his hand. His teeth grazed at her neck, then he clamped his lips on the skin, sucking back until she was crying out her orgasm.

Before she could relax, Quinn flipped her over on her knees and draped her upper body over the back of the couch. He lifted her skirt up, caressing her ass as he tugged down her panties. When she heard the sound of a foil wrapper ripping open, she couldn't help but giggle. "Always ready, huh? I thought you weren't a boy scout—uh!"

Quinn entered her in one thrust, and he steadied her by putting his hands on her hips. She groaned at the sensation of being so full. *So much better than my own fingers.*

"Are you okay, kitten?" he asked in a tense voice.

"Yeah ... don't ... stop now," she said, pushing back against him.

He let out a grunt and began to move in her. Short thrusts, at first, but soon he was swinging his hips and dragging his cock along her tight passage in long strokes.

She whimpered his name, the sensations making her unable to think of other words. Quinn hooked his fingers around her arms and pulled her up. A hand grabbed at the bottom of her shirt and untucked it from her skirt before slipping underneath the fabric. Deft fingers tugged down the cups of her bra and rolled the hardened nipples between the rough pads.

"You have the most gorgeous tits," he whispered into her ear.

"Keep going," she begged, pushing back against him and meeting his thrusts. "I'm almost ... ohhhh."

Quinn fucked into her faster, never losing the rhythm, even as his fingers left her nipples to snake down between her legs. When he pinched her clit, she cried out his name, her orgasm all hot and tingly as it washed over her entire body. She shook with pleasure, the words earth-shattering too weak to describe how she felt at her peak. Quinn wasn't far behind, and he thrust into her a couple more times before he let out a satisfied grunt, his cock twitching inside of her.

Selena's heart was beating at her ribcage like a sledgehammer, and the realization of what they had done began to creep into her semi-conscious mind. What had they done?

"Shit!" Quinn cursed as he slipped out of her.

She frowned and looked back at him as he struggled to zip up his pants. "Quinn?"

"Evie's here," he said, his head whipping toward the front door.

"How do you—" Right, super senses. Half a second later, the key turning the lock confirmed it.

Quinn bolted toward the bathroom, and Selena quickly straightened her skirt and pulled up her panties, adding a throw pillow on her lap for good measure. She sat back on the couch, trying to appear calm as Evie walked into the living room.

"Hey, Selena," Evie said, sitting down on the couch beside her. She wrinkled her nose at the empty pizza box. "You didn't leave any for me?"

"Sorry, I—"

The bathroom door opened and Quinn strolled out, his pants zipped up, and belt buckled. Evie's jaw dropped, and she looked at Selena.

"Hey, I fixed that leak in your bathroom," Quinn said, his

voice even as he looked at Selena. "See, I told you you didn't need a plumber."

Evie's eyes narrowed at Quinn. "You came here to fix a leak in our bathroom? Shouldn't our landlord take care of that?"

"Yeah, but he wasn't going to come in until tomorrow," Quinn said. "I had to make sure to plug the leak, at least."

Selena's eyes bulged at the comment, and it took all her strength not to start coughing and choking.

"Hey, thanks for the pizza, Selena," he said as he strolled to the door.

"I'll walk you out," she said hastily, getting to her feet. She followed Quinn to the front door, let him out first, and closed the door halfway. "Tonight was a mistake."

"Yeah, sure." He shrugged, shoving his hands in his pockets.

"This is the last time. This," she gestured between them, "is never going to happen again."

"Uh-huh," he said, tipping his chin up at her. "I agree. Never going to happen again." He turned and walked toward the stairs without another glance.

Selena closed the door behind her and let out a relieved sigh. Yes, definitely won't happen again.

13

"*T*his … is … the last time," Selena sighed.

"Yeah," Quinn agreed. "Definitely the last time. Ugh … move your hips like that."

"Oh, God."

Selena grabbed onto the headboard behind him and used the leverage to pump her hips down on him even harder, making Quinn groan in pleasure. He responded by popping a nipple into his mouth, scraping his teeth on the bud just enough to make it feel good.

"Quinn!" She rocked back faster, her thighs burning, but she didn't care. All she wanted was to come, and she was nearly there. God, he felt so good inside her.

"Selena, you're so beautiful," he mouthed against her breast.

The words made her heart melt. "Shut up," she said. "Don't make this weird."

"I'm not making this fucking weird," he snapped. "You are—"

She silenced him with her mouth, pushing her tongue past his lips and teeth. She wanted to taste him, fuck him, make him come. What she did not want was to feel so mushy inside when he said sweet things to her.

Her orgasm was approaching and, judging by the look on his face, Quinn was nearly there, too. She moved faster, lifting her hips up, so she could slam down hard on him. When her orgasm tore through her body, Quinn let out a groan and threw his head back as she clenched around him, his cock pumping inside her.

As soon as she regained control over her body, Selena rolled off him and got to her feet. Scanning around her, she began picking up her discarded clothing. How the hell did her panties end up all the way over there? She shook her head and grabbed the underwear from the corner of the flat screen TV and slipped it on.

"Heading out so soon, kitten?" Quinn asked.

She turned to face him. The infuriating man had his upper body propped up on the headboard, hands clasped behind his head, and a smirk plastered on his face. "I told you, this was the last time."

"Yeah, that's what you said yesterday. And the day before that. And—"

"All right, all right," she grumbled. "But I mean it this time."

"Uh-huh."

Selena put on her bra, skirt, and blouse, then walked down from his bedroom, making her way across the living space of his loft. Her shoes had been discarded near the couch, and she picked them up and slipped them onto her bare feet. As soon as she was out the door, she let out a sigh, finally able to breathe.

She truly had gone mental. That was the explanation for why, for a whole week now, she kept coming back to Quinn and having sex with him. It hadn't even been twenty-four hours since he left that night at her place when he came knocking on her door again. They barely made it out of the foyer.

She bit her lip. Why the hell was it so hard to say no to him? All he had to do was show up at her doorstep with that devastatingly handsome smile and boom! She was on her back. Or on top. Or on her knees. She let out an audible moan and slapped her hand over her eyes, as if that could block out the embarrassment she felt. Okay, so it wasn't always his doing. The other night, she was feeling particularly horny, and she might have, kind of, glanced over at Evie's phone when she left it on the sofa, and she might have, sort of, copied Quinn's number. She had, after all, something important to text him.

Hey, did you know that sex boosts your immune system? Send.

A moment later, she got a reply. *<Cough cough> I think I'm coming down with something. You should come up here now before it gets any worse. The Uber's on its way.* The message was followed by a link to the car that was on the way to pick her up and bring her to his place.

Selena shook her head, trying to get the memories out of her head. Walking to the elevator, she vowed to herself, for real this time, that she would never, ever have sex with Quinn again.

The cool air hit her face, and it felt refreshing. Being inside, surrounded by Quinn's scent and his maleness felt suffocating. A ring from her purse shook her out of her thoughts, and she fished for the phone inside.

"Great," she muttered seeing her father's name flash on the screen. She ignored it, not really wanting to talk to him right now. She knew what he wanted. A few seconds later a message popped up.

Have you made your decision? Call me.

Shit. Selena didn't want to have that discussion now. She rubbed her arms, feeling the cold chill seep into her skin. Dammit, she left her jacket upstairs. She pulled up the app for Uber and started typing in her address. She only hoped the driver would arrive before she froze to death.

Quinn watched Selena march out of the doorway in a huff. He hit the back of his head on the headboard. What the hell were they doing? No matter how hard he tried, he just kept coming back. And she didn't seem to mind either. Yet each time they finished the deed, she seemed even more distant. In those hours he lost himself in her, he thought he felt something, but then she'd pull back and leave him cold. This wasn't fair. This wasn't him. He was usually the one doing the leaving or the kicking out. Well, screw her (or not), he was not some sadist, and he wasn't going to keep going back for more. She was right. This would be the last time.

Wolf whined and growled.

"What now?" he asked in an irritated voice.

More whining and growling. God, it was like Wolf was obsessed with Selena. And the damned thing wouldn't leave him alone until he got up and started putting his clothes on.

"All right, you fucker," he said aloud. "I'm going, I'm going!" With a frustrated growl, he pulled his discarded shirt on, the fabric still smelling like Selena as she had, just an hour before, rubbed her naked tits all over his chest while they were making out on the couch. Ignoring the blood rushing to his cock, he jogged down the stairs as he slipped his shoes on. What the fuck was he doing, anyway? Selena would be long gone by now. She couldn't get out of his bed fast enough, after all, he thought bitterly. But this was the only way to show Wolf that Selena had no interest in them. Maybe then Quinn could get on with his life.

As he opened the door to his building, the cold spring air, as well as the subtle smell of butterscotch, hit his face. Standing with her back to him was Selena, her arms around herself, waiting by the sidewalk.

He seemed irresistibly drawn to her. "Selena," he called, placing his hands on her bare arms. The gooseflesh there indicated she was cold, and it took all his strength not to wrap his arms around her to keep the chill away.

She didn't move or struggle, but her body tensed. "What are you doing here?"

"Why don't you have your jacket on?" he countered.

"I ... couldn't find it," she said with a shrug.

"And you didn't go back up? Or call me?"

"I didn't think ... I mean, I ..." She turned around and looked up at him with those expressive blue-gray eyes. Right now, they seemed almost ... sorry? "I'm not handling this right. There's something I have to tell you—"

The lights of the car coming from his right were moving fast. Way too fast. He turned his head and realized that the headlights in the darkness were heading straight for them.

His instincts kicked in, and Quinn pushed Selena away. She let out an ear-piercing scream, and the force of the car made his body bounce against the hood and onto the sidewalk. Pain shot through his body. His vision was blurry, and he looked back at the car. There was a figure slumped over in the driver's seat, but he couldn't make out who it was. But that wasn't his priority right now. The smell of gasoline was overwhelming his heightened senses.

He let out a loud grunt and pushed himself up, managing to get away a few feet by the time he heard the explosion. Quinn's ears were ringing, and the heat from the fire was almost unbearable. But where was Selena? "Selena!" he screamed. At least he thought he was screaming. He was still deaf from the explosion. "Selena, where are you?" His heart tightened in his chest as the air grew hotter. Where was she? Did he push her away in time?

He felt the vibrations of stiletto heels on the pavement, and he turned to the source. Selena was there, and she was safe. He let out a sigh of relief.

"Quinn!" she cried as she knelt down next to him. "No, no, no, please!"

"Selena, are ... you ... okay?"

"Me?" she exclaimed as tears streaked down her face. "You just got hit by a car!"

"Don't cry," he said, reaching up to brush away the wetness from her cheeks. "It'll be fine." A sharp pain shot through him and he clutched at his side.

"Quinn!"

"I'm ... okay," he managed to get out. "Call ... Killian ..."

She nodded and then took her phone out. Quinn closed his eyes, trying to relax as he felt his body begin to knit itself back together. Accelerated healing was great to have, but it hurt like a bitch.

The minutes ticked by, but it seemed like hours to Quinn. Selena never left his side and continued to hold his hand the entire time. Finally, he felt the presence of other people around him, and he opened his eyes.

"Quinn?" Killian's face, full of worry, stared down at him. "How are you feeling?"

"Like I've been hit by a car," he said wryly. Killian let out a chuckle and helped him up. "Are we in trouble?"

"Hopefully not," Killian said. "This was an accident, right?"

Quinn looked at the remains of the wrecked car. The front was smashed against the wall, and the hood was charred. Inside, the figure was still slumped over the wheel. Shit. It was so close. Too close. Quinn was fine; he had Lycan healing, after all, but Selena ...

"Is she okay?" he asked in a panicked voice. "Where's Selena?"

Killian nodded behind him, and Quinn turned around. He

blinked several times. "Shit, that explosion must have knocked my brain out. I'm seeing double." There were two redheads in the corner, talking softly.

"You are seeing double." Killian chuckled. "That's the Beta's wife, Cady Vrost. She's here to smooth things over with the authorities."

"Oh crap." He looked around. Nick Vrost, Beta to the New York Clan, was talking to a couple of police officers. "Fuck."

"Well, what do you think?"

It was an accident, wasn't it? Because who would want to run over some random person, kamikaze style? Whoever had driven that car was dead. But, still, there was a small part of him screaming that something was wrong. "I don't know, Killian."

14

Selena was almost nervous when Cady Vrost approached her. For one thing, she must have looked terrible. Her hair was tangled, her top was torn, and she was pretty sure she had a nasty scrape on her thighs from when she hit the pavement. Cady, on the other hand, looked perfect with her coppery red hair up in a French twist and her expensive-looking skirt suit. Still, she couldn't very well ignore New York clan's Human Liaison and her distant cousin.

"Hi, Selena Merlin, right?" Cady asked as she held out her hand. "I'm—"

"Cady Gray. I mean, Vrost," Selena corrected herself. "I know you. I mean, I know of you."

Cady raised a graceful brow. "Really?"

"Yeah, we're related. I mean, sort of. Distantly. My great-great-great-great er ... I'm not sure if that's enough 'greats,' but anyway ... I'm also related to Charlotte Fontaine on my mother's side."

"Oh!" Cady exclaimed and, instead of shaking her hand, drew Selena in for a hug. "Nice to meet you then, Selena. And you're a witch," she said, releasing her from the hug. "This makes my job much easier."

"Er, technically, I'm not a witch, but yes," Selena nodded, "I know about Lycans, and you don't have to send me off with a dose of confusion potion."

She chuckled. "Right. Well, can you tell me what you're doing here and what happened?"

"Er ..."

"Selena! Are you all right?" Meredith exclaimed as she approached the pair.

Great timing. Selena turned to the Lycan. "I'm fine, just shaken, and I kind of kissed the pavement trying to get out of the way." She raised her hands to show the scratches on them.

Meredith took her hands excitedly and scrutinized them. Her brows knitted together then she looked at Selena's face. "Your forehead."

"Oh, crap." Selena touched her left temple gingerly and winced when she felt the lump and scratches on the skin. It wasn't bleeding, thank God, but she was going to feel it for a while. "Maybe I should go to the emergency room."

"You shouldn't have to ..." Meredith muttered. She glanced over to where Quinn was talking to Killian and Nick, and then back to Selena. "Are you sure you're ... okay?"

Selena shrugged. "I mean, I can walk and stuff. It was the fall that hurt me more. Quinn managed to push me out of the way before the car hit us. But I'll live."

"So, what were you doing here?" Meredith asked, her eyes narrowing at Selena. "Outside Quinn's apartment?"

"I ... we were coming back from dinner," Selena lied. "I walked him back, and my Uber was going to pick me up here."

"Is that so?" Meredith sniffed at her. "Hmmm, you smell like gasoline and concrete."

"Well duh, a car exploded six feet away from me."

"Wait, are you still a virgin?"

"Meredith!" Selena cried. She could feel the heat in her cheeks, clearly showing how embarrassed she was by the question. "What does that have to do with this?"

Cady cleared her throat politely. "Um, Selena, are you sure you're okay? I can have our doctor check you over if you'd rather not have anyone asking questions."

Selena looked around them. A crowd was already starting to gather outside the barriers the NYPD had erected. "I think I'm fine. I'll just head home. My roommate is probably worried."

"We can have our car take you home," Cady said, taking her phone out of her purse.

"That would be great," Selena said with a sigh, not having the strength to protest. "Can I go and say goodbye to Quinn first?"

Cady nodded. Selena left her and Meredith, then turned toward where Quinn was still talking to Killian. Her heart pounded in her chest, but the ache in her stomach was gone now, especially when she saw Quinn up and about. Seeing him hit by the car and lying on the pavement had torn her apart, and she still felt the tears welling up in her eyes when imagining Quinn's body. She had to see that he was all right and then ... then maybe she really needed to be firmer in her resolve to not sleep with him again. And next time she was tempted? Well, she'd have to continue with what she was trying to do just before the runaway car interrupted them. Tell him the truth. She figured he would hate her, but at least he would stay away if he knew she was considering getting engaged.

"Quinn," she called softly.

Quinn went very still and then slowly pivoted. His blue eyes seemed to glow in the darkness, scanning every inch of her.

"I'm all right," she said when he moved a step toward her. He raised a hand to touch her face. "Please," she whispered, her voice barely audible. "Everyone's here. Watching."

He gritted his teeth and then dropped his hand. "Are you really okay?"

"I'm fine. A little bruised." She paused. "Thank you for saving my life."

He nodded, his jaw tense. "Of course. Are you headed home?"

"Yes, Cady Vrost is having a car take me to my apartment."

"I have to stay and sort this out." He sighed. "Just message me when you're in bed, okay?"

"I will." With one last glance at him, she turned away and began to walk back to Cady and Meredith.

She stayed a few more minutes to answer some questions from the police officers on the scene. When they told her she could go, Cady helped her get into the car. The drive back to her apartment was mercifully quick. Evie had been waiting up for her. Selena didn't know Killian's number, so she had called Evie who then called Killian. She was too tired to tell her what happened, but accepted her comforting hugs and help getting out of her dirty and ripped clothes. Selena texted an *"I'm home"* message to Quinn before collapsing in bed.

---

*Q*uinn stared at the report on the screen, reading it over and over again. The Beta was able to get a copy of the detective's initial findings on the incident and sent it over to Lone Wolves.

The authorities were ruling it an accident. Apparently, the man who had run them over, Jon Dover, was seen leaving a bar a few blocks away from the scene drunk as a skunk. Witnesses said Dover had been drinking all night before he stumbled out the door. The Medical Examiner's report wasn't in yet, but he would get it as soon as it was ready.

Still, no one had seen Dover get into his car. There were no cameras on the street that caught him entering his vehicle (or none that were functioning). Quinn had hacked into a couple of cameras around the area, including one that monitored the outside of his building, but they only showed the vehicle speeding down the street and then heading straight for them.

He should just call it a day. It was a freak accident. But there was something not right about the whole thing. So, he reached out to a couple of contacts on a private network—people who could help him do things that were not quite on the right side of the law. It might take a while, but he would get the information he needed eventually. Until he was one hundred percent sure it wasn't an accident, he wouldn't be able to breathe easy.

Quinn leaned back in his chair and rubbed his eyes. He'd been working on this for two days now. The day after the accident, he went to work, barely eating or sleeping, to find out what happened. Wolf was not happy, but he told the animal he needed to know if anyone was trying to hurt Selena, and that seemed to quiet down the beast. He thought of looking into Selena's background to see if someone was after her, but that would be an invasion of her privacy. If it turned out it wasn't an accident, then he'd go ahead and ask her. But for now ...

"Jesus," he muttered softly, looking at the clock. It was dark outside, and he didn't even notice. His stomach grumbled, and he realized he hadn't eaten in a couple of hours. His thoughts went to Selena, wondering where she was. If she were hurt, she'd tell him, right? Or Evie would. Quinn tended to be consumed by his work, especially when he was racing to find out what happened before a trail went cold. Plus, if he was in danger, it was better to stay away from Selena, no matter how much he wanted to hold her and make sure she was okay. Wolf growled when his thoughts strayed to Selena, the animal obviously unhappy about being away from its favorite person.

"All right!" He shot up from his chair impatiently. He thought of calling or texting her to see what was up, but she might turn him away. All those times he did show up at her place with food and beer, well, they ended up in bed. If Selena invited him to have sex, he wasn't exactly going to say no. Maybe it could be his lucky night again.

---

15

*S*elena plopped down on the couch, getting ready to watch a sad, sappy romance. Normally, this wasn't her style, but her damn hormones demanded a good cry. She woke up this morning, feeling achy in her lower back (and not just from the accident) and lo and behold, Aunt Flo had arrived. Yup, it was that time of the month. Shark Week. She hated getting her period, but it was something she had to suffer through. Thank goodness she wasn't one of those girls with debilitating periods, but it certainly put her system out of whack.

Being on the rag was also a good reason why she had been irritable all day. It couldn't be because Quinn hadn't contacted her in two days. Two whole days. Maybe he was done with her. Shaking her head, she turned back to the movie.

A few scenes (and a whole bunch of tissues) into the movie, the doorbell rang. Who could that be? Evie was gone for a couple of days, having gone back to Kansas City for her father's birthday. She paused the movie and walked to the front door.

"Quinn?" she squeaked when she saw who it was through

the peephole. She quickly opened the door. "What are you doing here?"

"I came to—Jesus, what's the matter?"

"Huh?" Selena frowned.

"Have you been crying?" he asked, his voice edgy. "Who made you cry? Are you hurt? Have you been to the doctor?"

"Oh, crap." She realized that she must have looked horrendous. Her nose was probably red, her eyes swollen, and her skin blotchy. "No, I'm fine ... I was just watching a sad movie."

"A sad movie made you cry?" he asked in a skeptical voice.

"I'm on my period, okay?" she blurted out.

"Oh."

Selena bit her lip. "Yeah, so sorry, I'm not, uh, up to entertaining. Down there, I mean." She gave herself a mental slap on the forehead. "I mean, it's probably like a murder scene in my vagina." Holy shit, did she just say vagina? In front of Quinn? *Shit. Quit while you're ahead, girl.* "So, yeah, maybe I'll talk to you soon, yeah?" And with that, she closed the door on Quinn's surprised face.

She stood there for a couple minutes, listening to Quinn's retreating footsteps. When she was sure he was gone, she breathed a sigh of relief and walked back to the couch. If she had kept babbling on about her bloody (pun intended) vagina, she'd probably die of embarrassment. Now Quinn would never want to touch her again. Not that she wanted him to. Reflecting on the whole situation gave her some much needed clarity. She would end things with Quinn now, while it didn't hurt yet. While she still had the strength to walk away.

The ring of the buzzer jolted Selena out of her thoughts. "What?" she said aloud. Who was it this time? She got up and walked back to the foyer. Not bothering to check the peephole, she opened the door a crack. "Quinn?"

"Hey, Selena," he said, placing his hand on the door and

giving it a gentle push. The door gave way, and he strode into the foyer.

"Quinn, what are you doing? I thought I told you ... I'm indisposed."

"Yeah, I understand you're on the rag, jeez, I'm not dumb," Quinn said, rolling his eyes. He held up the large paper bag in his other hand. "That's why I got you these."

"What did you get me?" she asked, confused.

"Here," he shoved it into her arms. "I walked to the pharmacy around the corner and got you a couple things."

Curious, Selena opened the bag. The item on top was an electric heating pad. Then there were about a dozen different chocolate bars. But what made her laugh out loud was the boxes of feminine hygiene products. There were about half a dozen brands buried at the bottom of the bag.

"Tampons? And pads?" she asked, barely able to keep her face straight. "You bought all these? For me?"

"Yeah, I wasn't sure I got the right ones. Meredith was always so picky," he said with a moan. "It was always 'that's not what I use' or 'that one's not comfortable' or 'it's the third Sunday when Venus is crossing over Saturn, so I only use this brand.'"

"Wait ... Meredith made you buy her tampons and pads?" Selena bit her lip to keep from bursting out with laughter.

"She was one of those girls who couldn't move when she had her period, you know?" Quinn explained. "So, each month, Killian, Connor, and I would have to take turns on who would get her stuff."

Selena burst out laughing, the first real one she'd had in a while. "I can't ... I can't ..." Tears were pooling in her eyes. "I can't imagine Connor pawing through boxes of tampons in the drug store!" The image alone made her crack up.

"Ha!" Quinn chuckled. "Believe it or not, Connor always got the right ones. I'm the one who always had to go back and find the correct brand." He scratched his head. "I think she was messing with me."

"I ... I ..." The laughter made it hard to form words, but when she finally calmed down, she let out a sigh. "I stock my own feminine hygiene products, FYI," she said.

"Good to know. Let's go to the couch. We can keep watching your movie, and I'll plug in the heating pad. Maybe you can scarf down all that chocolate until you feel better."

He moved toward the living room, but she stopped him with a hand on the chest. "Wait," she said. "You want to come in? And watch sappy movies with me?"

"I got nothing else to do," he said with a shrug.

"But you know I can't ... I mean ... down there." Her cheeks heated. Oh God, she was going to die of mortification.

"Are you twelve, Selena?" Quinn asked in an impatient voice. "I know how stuff works down there. You don't have to be embarrassed you're on your period. Now," he took her by the shoulders and pushed her to the side. "I'm gonna order some Chinese food for dinner. You go and do what you need to do to get comfy." He walked into the living room, leaving a dumbfounded Selena in the foyer.

*A*s he promised, Quinn ate dinner and watched the movie with her, never making fun of her or mocking the overly melodramatic scenes. He simply handed her a tissue each time she started weeping. When he saw that she looked uncomfortable trying to squeeze herself on the other end of the couch, he gestured for her to come into his side. She curled up against his warm body, sighing as he positioned the heating pad on her aching lower back.

When the credits rolled, Selena looked up at Quinn's face.

He was very still, his eyes closed. He looked so different to her when he was like this. Handsome, yes, but the quiet strength she never knew was inside him seemed to shine through. The night of the accident, she had experienced that intensity, just not physically. While she had broken down and panicked, he had been calm, despite being in so much pain. Of course, she knew Lycans had accelerated healing, but, in that moment, she had thought he was going to die and she was going to lose him. Tears welled up in her eyes again, not from the movie but real ones that sent a tightness through her chest.

She took a deep breath to stop the tears and attempted to disentangle herself from Quinn. Tried to, anyway, because when she went to shimmy out of his arms, he just scooped her up and planted her on his lap, making her legs straddle him.

"Hi there," he said with a sleepy, boyish smile, as he opened his eyes.

"Hi there," she said back, reaching up to push a lock of blond hair that had fallen over his forehead. The air went very still and quiet. Even the noise of the city seemed to fade away as Quinn pulled her down to press his lips to hers. She sighed, opening up her mouth to him. He tasted like the chocolate bars they had shared. She could also feel the growing bulge pressing up against her stomach.

"Uh, sorry," he said, pulling away. "I can't help it." He ran his hands down her back and over her ass. "You're so sexy, and you smell so good." He nuzzled at her neck, making her moan aloud and rub herself on him. "Kitten," he gasped. "You gotta stop or else."

Selena had a naughty thought. Well, she always had wicked thoughts around Quinn, but this one was very naughty. "Or what?" she asked, sliding off his lap and onto the floor. She got on her knees and spread his legs apart.

A golden brow raised at her. "Selena?"

"Hmmm?" she asked, her eyes never leaving the bulge in his crotch. She traced her hand over it, pressing down as her palm ran over the ridge of his erection.

"Selena ..."

"Take off your shirt," she said. She wanted to see his sexy chest and abs, as well as his taut golden skin and his tattoo. Plus, she didn't want him to ruin his clothes.

Quinn obliged, whipping the tight black t-shirt over his head. He looked down at her, desire burning in his eyes. "Your turn. Show me those gorgeous tits, kitten."

She unbuttoned her blouse, slowly, until she was kneeling in front of him in just her bra. Reaching behind her, she unclasped her bra and let it fall to the floor. The exposed nipples immediately tightened under his gaze.

"Nice," he said, his eyes never leaving her breasts.

She swallowed a gulp but continued, scrunching up every bit of courage. Her fingers found the fly of his jeans and popped the buttons one by one, then tugged at his pants and underwear. Quinn lifted his hips so she could pull them all the way down to his ankles. His cock stood at attention, and Selena felt apprehensive. Despite all the times they'd been together, she'd never done *this*. Quinn never pressured or even asked her to give him oral, and she was relieved because she would hate to be a disappointment.

Sensing her hesitation, Quinn spoke. "Selena, you don't have to do this," he said, though his voice was strained. "You're not—ugh!"

Her hand grasped around the base of his cock. "But I want to," she said, looking up at him as she opened her mouth and took the tip into it. Quinn bucked his hips up, and he let out a pained groan.

Selena wished she had at least read up on what she was supposed to do, but she supposed she could take a chapter from his book and just copy what he's done for her in the past. So, she swirled her tongue around the bulbous head. Hmmm ... Quinn was moaning now, so it was probably good. She gripped his cock harder and then began to slide her mouth down on his shaft slowly, as he was not exactly a small man.

"Fuck! Selena!" His hands dug into her hair, fingers curling around the locks gently. He pulled her up, and she followed his lead, sliding her mouth up and down his shaft, teasing the underside with the rough pad of her tongue.

"Selena ... shit ... I'm gonna come ..."

Selena clamped her mouth around him harder, her hands gripped the base as she felt his cock spasm. Quinn grunted and pulled himself from her mouth as thick cum began to shoot from his cock. He placed his hand over hers and tugged back on his shaft, causing the cum to spurt all over his chest and stomach.

"Shit ... kitten ..." He looked down and let out a small laugh. "You made a mess."

"I made a mess?" she asked with a chuckle. "You need better aim." She stood up and put her hands on her hips. "What am I going to do with you?" She sighed.

"For starters, you can get me a towel. I don't wanna stain your couch," he said. "Then you can sit on my lap, and I can suck on those nipples."

"Don't move," she said, heading into the bathroom. She came out with a damp towel and stood over him.

He took the towel from her hands. "Thanks." He cleaned himself off, dropped the towel on the floor, and then tugged her down on his lap.

"Hey," she giggled, "I gotta go and put your jizz towel in the hamper."

"Jizz towel?" He laughed. "Well, I suppose it'll be my towel now."

"Yeah, I don't think Evie will want her washcloth back," she said. "Quinn!" she cried when his warm mouth encircled a nipple. "Quinn ... I want to ... but we can't." *Stupid Aunt Flo.*

He nipped at her bud lightly. "Kitten," he said, "We don't have to go all the way." He slid a hand between them, dipping lower, under her leggings and panties. "There are other ways, you know." She gasped when his finger rubbed over her clit, but it never strayed lower. "Besides, I read that orgasms were the best way to relieve cramps."

She bit her lip and pushed her hips at his fingers. "We should keep that jizz towel handy then."

He laughed.

Quinn shifted uncomfortably on the narrow mattress. Selena was not kidding when she said they had twin beds in the bedroom. For them to fit in one bed, Selena had to squeeze up against the wall and he had to lie on his side. Still, that also meant she was pressed up against him all night long, and he loved feeling the soft curves of her body, especially her plush ass. He groaned as his cock started to get hard again. He already came twice last night, yet he was still horny.

Selena moaned and twisted around, nearly knocking him off the bed. He steadied himself, and she buried her face into his chest, rubbing her nose on him. Now her naked tits were smashed against his chest, and he could feel her nipples grazing his skin. Jeez, this wasn't much better. When was he going to stop wanting her all the damn time? He was counting the days until she was better and he could drive right into her again ...

He pushed those thoughts aside and looked over at the other bed. Quinn supposed that he would be much more comfortable on the other bed, but he doubted Evie would appreciate that, especially after what he did to her washcloth. Quinn chuckled, thinking about how he wanted to burn the damn thing, but Selena insisted on keeping the jizz towel as a souvenir.

He let out a heavy sigh and closed his eyes. He wasn't sure what was going to happen after this, but he did know he wasn't going to stay away from Selena. After the accident, when he thought she was hurt or worse, he almost lost it. He had to break down her walls and convince her that they were good together. And whatever *together* meant, they could figure out later.

*Q*uinn thought the best way to show Selena that they should be together was to stick with her as much as possible. For the next couple days, he picked her up at the library as soon as she was done at work and then went home with her. It was a good thing Evie decided to extend her visit to Kansas because—hooray—that meant more blow jobs. But he was getting tired of squeezing into the twin bed with Selena. He didn't dare suggest they go back to his place because whenever they were out in public together, she seemed nervous and wouldn't even hold his hand. They seemed like purely platonic friends whenever they were out.

"Burgers or Japanese?" Quinn asked as he strolled up to her desk.

"Burgers," she said without looking up from her computer. "But I want ice cream afterward, too."

"Whatever you want, kitten."

Selena closed up her computer and followed him out of the library. They went to a burger place around the corner where the food was good and reasonably priced (at least for New York).

Afterward, Selena insisted they take the subway uptown to an ice cream shop.

"You already paid for dinner," Selena said. "You need to stop spending money on me and do something more useful with your cash. Your rent alone must be a fortune. I don't even want to think about how much you've spent on Uber with your credit cards."

Quinn bit back a retort. None of the other girls he went out with cared if he were spending too much money on them. In fact, many of them demanded it. Yet, here was Selena, worried about his credit score. He chuckled to himself and wondered if he should tell her how rich he was. Not billionaire rich, of course, but he was certainly flush enough to take her on all the Uber rides she wanted.

"Fine, whatever you want." The traffic in the city would be horrible anyway, and the subway made more sense. They took the train to the Upper West Side and walked to the ice cream shop. There was a long line outside, and, although Quinn rolled his eyes, he followed Selena to the end of the queue. She seemed excited about having ice cream, so he couldn't disappoint her.

"What is this place?" he asked.

"They just opened a week ago. They specialize in alcoholic ice cream," Selena said with a sparkle in her eye.

"Oh, is that so?" he asked. "Are you trying to get me drunk on ice cream? So you can take advantage of me?"

She let out a laugh. "There's not enough liquor in the ice cream to get anyone drunk, much less a Lycan."

"All right, lady," he chuckled. "But I'm watching you. You better keep your hands to yourself."

They waited in line patiently, and it went by faster than he anticipated. As they stood there, Selena's phone rang a few times, but she ignored it. After a few more rings, she finally turned it off with an annoyed huff. Who the hell could be calling her over and over again? A weird feeling settled over him, but he ignored it as they reached the front of the line.

Selena got an Irish cream flavored ice cream with sprinkles, while Quinn opted for one made with chocolate stout and pretzel bits. They stood outside the shop, leaning against the wall as they enjoyed their ice cream, Quinn finishing his in three bites.

"Want a taste?" Selena asked, offering him her cone.

"Sure," he said. As she pushed her cone at him, he grabbed her wrist and pulled her to him instead. He was taking a risk and it might scare her away, but, why not? He caught her lips with his, savoring the cold and sweet taste of her mouth as she opened to him. The ice cream cone dropped to the ground, but when he tried to pull away, she snaked her arms around his neck instead and pulled him closer. Pushing her up against the wall, he buried his hands in her hair and angled her head so he could slant his mouth over hers and slide his tongue into her mouth.

"Quinn," she whispered as he pulled away.

He leaned his forehead against her and opened his eyes. "Sorry about the ice cream. I'll get you another one."

"No," she said. "Take me home? To your place, I mean."

His heart thudded in his chest. "Are you sure?" Maybe she was coming around and getting used to this *together* thing.

She nodded. "Evie's back home. And ... Aunt Flo is gone."

"Who?" He paused, then realized what she was saying. "Oh. Why didn't you tell me right away?"

"Would you have taken me for ice cream?" she asked cheekily, which earned her a nip on the ear. "Quinn," she moaned when his tongue snaked out to lick the shell of her ear.

"I would have taken you for ice cream ... eventually. I can't wait to be inside you," he said, pressing his lower body to hers. He was already half hard, thinking about sliding into her.

"Then what are we waiting for?" she asked.

Quinn took her hand and dragged her down to the corner. "Dammit," he cursed when two cabs went past them. He took out his phone. No Ubers anywhere near them, either.

"It's rush hour. We'll never get a cab," she said. "Let's take the subway; it'll be faster anyway."

"Fine," he growled. Besides, he wasn't sure if he could control himself if they were in the back of a car. He wanted her now.

They walked two blocks to the nearest subway station that would take them downtown to Quinn's loft. After getting Quinn a MetroCard, they walked through the turnstiles to the main train platform.

As they stood on the platform, Quinn suddenly felt uneasy. The desire and impatience he was feeling had ebbed away, but not because he didn't want Selena. No, the hairs on the back of his neck were raised, and he felt like he was being watched. He glanced around, but there were so many people, he couldn't be sure.

The train arrived, and they moved inside one of the cramped cars, but, still, the feeling wouldn't go away. He put an arm protectively around Selena, and when she looked up at him with her brows knitted, he gave her a tight smile. No need to worry her, especially if he was just being paranoid.

They had to switch at Times Square, which was probably a mistake. The platform was hot and crowded and filled with annoyed New Yorkers coming home from work and confused tourists looking at paper maps or gawking all around.

Quinn tuned out the din of the crowd and concentrated on the sounds from the rail. Using his enhanced senses, he heard the incoming train, even before there was an announcement over the speakers. Knowing that the train would be pulling in any time, he moved them closer to the edge, so they would be the first ones in.

"Quinn, you're so impatient," she joked.

He didn't answer her because the hairs on the back of his neck were bristling now and Wolf stood at attention. A low, rumbling growl ripped from his chest, which took Selena aback.

"Quinn? What's wrong?" Her eyes were wide, searching his face for an answer. "Are you—"

It all went by fast. Too fast. He saw a figure in a gray hoodie rush behind Selena as they fell backward. The man's face was obscured by his hoodie, and Quinn scented the air, trying to identify something because there was no way a human could move that fast. The other Lycan smelled of dirt and something pungent, like mildew.

The air knocked out of him as he landed on the subway rails, Selena on top of him. Someone screamed, and lights were coming in fast to their right. Wolf growled and snarled in warning.

"Shit!" he cursed, then sprang into action. Quinn lifted Selena into his arms, jumped to his feet and leaped to the platform. The train missed them by inches, and the force from the rushing air knocked them forward.

"Jesus Christ!" someone screamed.

"Ow! Get off me!"

"What the fuck?"

Quinn and Selena barreled into a group of tourists, landing on top of them. He quickly got up, pulling Selena with him. "Where the fuck is he?" he roared, looking around for the Lycan in the hoodie. But there was no sign of him. "Shit!" He sniffed the air, finding a small trace of the scent. Wolf perked up, urging him to go after him.

He dragged Selena by the hand, across the platform, and up

the stairs. By the time they reached the outside of the station, the scent was gone.

"Fuck!" He slammed a fist against a wall. He had gotten away.

"Quinn," Selena said, taking deep breaths. "What the fuck is going on?"

"Shit," he said, running his fingers through his hair. "I'll explain later." He looked around the street and spotted a cab coming toward them. "Let's go to Killian's place. He'll need to hear about this."

---

*T*he cab took them across town to the East side, in the Kips Bay area of Midtown. Quinn had fired off messages on his phone the whole ride over as Selena sat silently beside him. She wasn't sure if her heart was ever going to stop racing like a horse at the Kentucky Derby, but as she curled up against Quinn's side, she felt a sense of calm, especially when she breathed in his aftershave. Quinn cuddled her closer but said nothing, his body rigid and stiff.

Something was very wrong, but if they were going to his brother's place, she would find out what soon enough. When they arrived at the condo, it looked like Killian was already expecting them. He opened the door and led them inside. Luna was sitting on the leather couch, while Connor stood by the window across the living room, his face drawn into a scowl.

"Quinn! Selena!" Luna exclaimed as she struggled to get up. "What happened? Are you guys okay?"

Selena quickly strode over to her and gently stopped her. "We're fine. Please, don't get up." She sat next to her, and Luna put an arm around her.

"Are you all right? Killian said you guys fell off the subway platform?" Luna asked.

"More like pushed off," Quinn said, his expression tight with barely controlled anger.

It had happened so fast, Selena could barely remember. She closed her eyes. "I think ... there was someone who pushed my back and sent us tumbling into the rails."

"It was a Lycan."

"Are you sure?" Killian asked.

"Yeah," Quinn confirmed. "I smelled him. Like mildew and dirt."

"Did you see his face?" Connor asked.

Quinn shook his head. "No, he had a hoodie pulled over his face and there were too many people." His fists tightened at his sides. "I swear, if I see or smell the sonofabitch again, I'm going to kill him."

Selena felt a chill creep up her arms at the deadliness in Quinn's voice.

"We'll ask for the clan's help in identifying the Lycan," Killian said. "Maybe if someone recognizes the scent, then we can find this guy."

"I don't think the wreck the other night was an accident," Quinn said.

Selena gasped. "What do you mean?"

"One incident I could ignore, but two?" Quinn shook his head. "Someone's out to get me."

"Or Selena," Killian pointed out. "You were together both times." Killian's turquoise gaze zeroed in on her. "Would you know anyone who's trying to hurt you?"

She shook her head. "Certainly not. I mean, not a Lycan."

"Your coven doesn't have enemies?"

"None that I know of," Selena began. "Most covens get along with each other. Marriages and alliances tend to strengthen the bond in the magical community." Thoughts of her possible engagement popped into her head, but she ignored it. "And, as for Lycans, we keep tabs on where they are and who their Alpha is, but we try to stay out of their way."

"Still, it might be good to look into your background."

"Excuse me?" she said, raising her voice. "You will do no such thing." No one was going to paw through her private life, especially not Quinn and his brothers. She looked at Quinn, wondering what his reaction would be.

"She's right," Quinn said. When Killian tried to speak, he raised a hand. "No, Killian. Selena has a right to her privacy."

"Thank you," Selena whispered in a relieved tone.

"I'm going to keep digging into the accident and maybe find some footage on the platform to see if we can spot this guy."

"But what about Selena? What if someone is after her?" Luna asked in a worried voice.

"I'll keep her safe," Quinn said. "She'll stay with me from now on."

"What?" Selena shot to her feet. "I'm not going to live with you!"

"Well, if you won't let us dig into your background to see if someone is trying to hurt you, then you need to be protected at all times. Besides, if someone has been following me, they know where you live by now since I've been going home with you for the past couple of days."

Luna tilted her head and narrowed her eyes at Selena. "Oh, is he?"

Selena ignored her. "Maybe I should stay away from you, then," she challenged. "They don't want me."

"Or they could use you to get to Quinn," Luna pointed out.

"It's settled then," Quinn announced. "You're going to stay with me until we find whoever is out to get us."

Selena's jaw dropped, and she looked at Luna, Killian, even

Connor, begging with her eyes for them to protest on her behalf. When no one spoke, she let out a heavy sigh. "Fine. But that means my house isn't safe, either. Evie just got home today, so she's all alone." She put on a smug smile. "Maybe she can stay with Quinn, too."

"Connor will look out for her," Quinn countered.

"What?" Connor growled. "Evie can't stay with me."

"Jeez, don't get your panties in a twist. I just mean, make sure she's safe while she's out and about. The security in their building is pretty solid, and I can even install an alarm system or a camera to monitor the front door. Evie should probably have a panic button of some sort, anyway, since she's working for us."

Connor looked at Killian, who nodded. He let out a curse under his breath. "Fine."

"Good, it's settled then. Quinn, you take Selena home and Connor, go and see if Evie's okay." As Connor turned to leave, Killian called out. "Don't scare her, okay? Knock on the door and make sure she's inside. Tell her what happened."

"She might be worried if I don't come home," Selena added. "Please tell her I'm fine."

Connor grunted in agreement and then left.

"What do we need to do to find out who's after you?" Killian asked, his voice grave.

"I'll take care of it," Quinn replied. "And when I need you guys ..."

"We'll be there."

---

*S*elena still couldn't believe she had somehow been conned into staying with Quinn. "Are you kidding me?" she hissed at him as they left Killian's place.

"What?" he said with a shrug. "Now we don't have to sneak around. You have a legit, life-or-death reason to stay over at my place."

"That's not the point!"

"Then what is?" He grabbed her by the shoulders. "Selena, you could have been killed." His voice was deadly serious.

"And you could've, too," she countered.

"I'm a Lycan," he pointed out. "Look, I can't just stand by and wait for someone to hurt you. Luna's right. Whoever's trying to get to me has seen you two times now."

She let out a sigh. "All right. When do you think you'll find this guy?"

"I'm doing my best to finish this quickly."

"Fine," she said. "Let's go to your place then. I can ask Evie to bring me a change of clothes when she comes in tomorrow."

He breathed a sigh of relief. "Great, let's go home."

She followed him as he hailed a cab, and then they were on their way. Selena didn't know why, but the way he said the word 'home' made her heart ache. A home with Quinn? That concept seemed alien somehow, but also ... She shook her head. No, she wouldn't go down that path. Whatever they were, it wasn't going to last. They were having fun now, and when he got tired of her, he would leave her. When the next pretty face came along, he would drop her, just like all those other boys did. Quinn was a nice person, and he wanted to protect her from danger. That was all. Once it was over, they wouldn't even have a reason to hang out.

The cab arrived in record time, and Quinn helped her out. Then they took the elevator up to his loft. As soon as they entered, he pushed her up against the door. "Now, kitten," he said, his generous mouth spreading into a lascivious smile. "Where were we?"

$\mathcal{W}$ aking up with Selena in his arms was possibly the best feeling in the entire world. Well, second best, Quinn thought. First was being inside her, though he would keep that fact to himself. He wanted to have sex with her the whole night, but Selena looked tired. She'd had a long day, after all. They both did. The incident at the subway platform only cemented his suspicions that the car wreck the other night was a deliberate attempt on his life. Still, who would go through so much trouble to make his death look like an accident?

That's what puzzled Quinn the most. He'd worked with some pretty nasty people in the past. When he did jobs, he didn't exactly stop and check everyone's resumes. But, most of those people wouldn't try to cover up his death and make it look like an accident. No one would bother. After all, he was inconsequential. Aside from his siblings, no one else in the world would care if he died.

He rose from the bed, nudging Selena gently. "It's seven, kitten," he whispered. She rolled onto her back and put the pillow over her head.

"No ..." she moaned.

He chuckled. "Time to get to work." And yes, he had work to do, as well. He had to get to the bottom of this.

Selena grumbled and then tossed the pillow onto the floor. But she got up anyway and headed into the bathroom.

After they both got dressed (Selena tried to get frisky in the shower, but he reminded her that it was a workday), they left the loft and headed over to the Lone Wolf office. Evie was already there, and she gave Quinn a dirty look as she passed a duffel bag to Selena.

"Thanks, I'll go change," Selena said, grabbing the bag from Evie and walking out the door.

"Wait, a minute," Evie called after her. "I need to talk to you."

"Evie!" Killian called. "Can you come in here, please?"

Evie looked at the hallway leading to Killian's office and back to Selena. "We'll talk later." As she passed by Quinn, she flashed him another angry look and disappeared down the hallway.

"I'll call you an Uber," he said to Selena. "And text me as soon as you get to the library. Don't leave after work until I'm there, okay? I'll be by early, and I'll wait for you outside."

"Fine," Selena said with a pout. "I'll see you later."

Quinn sighed, watching as the front door closed and Selena was gone. There was a tightness in his chest now that she wasn't around. Maybe he should go after her and make sure she was safe. Knowing there was someone out there who may be trying to get to him by harming Selena was making him and Wolf uneasy. Having Selena around helped calm down the animal, but, until she was safe, he would always feel worried. Selena was put at risk twice now, and Wolf wanted to hurt someone, preferably whoever it was trying to kill him.

With a long sigh, he walked to his office and shut the door. It would be a long day, and he wasn't going to give up until he put a stop to this entire thing.

---

*S*elena watched the hand on the clock tick by, counting the seconds. Had it only been five minutes since she last checked the time? She thought it had been much longer. It wasn't even lunch time yet.

"Damn you, clock," she muttered under her breath. Was five p.m. never going to come? "Arrgghhhh." She slumped back in her chair.

As she left Quinn's office this morning, her chest felt like lead—heavy and unforgiving. There was something not quite right with Quinn. For starters, he didn't even try to get her to round two last night, despite claiming he'd been waiting all week to be inside her. After they had sex, he simply pulled her to his chest and rubbed her back, which only made her sleepy. It felt nice, but orgasms were much nicer. She thought he must have been tired, so she yawned and soon gave in to sleep herself. And this morning, he was acting all strange and antsy. It was like he couldn't wait to get out of his apartment.

She let out a puff of breath. Was Quinn already getting tired of her? She expected it to happen, but not this soon. Maybe he realized she wasn't worth all this trouble.

"Dammit!" She got to her feet and grabbed her purse. He said he would come back for her after work, but she couldn't wait. It was almost lunch anyway. Her resolve in place, Selena walked to Lone Wolf Security. Thanks to her brisk pace, she got there in record time.

She took the ancient elevator and went up to the door, knocking on the glass sharply with her knuckles.

"Selena," Evie said when she opened the door. Her best friend placed a hand on her hip. "Back so soon?"

Selena stepped into the office. "Where is he?"

"In there." Evie jerked her thumb toward Quinn's office. "Hey what are you—"

She ignored Evie and marched to the second door down the hallway. "Quinn," she called when she entered. "Quinn!"

"Huh?" A blond head popped over the three monitors set up on the table in the middle of the room. Quinn's eyes widened in surprise, then narrowed. "Selena, what are you doing here?"

He did not sound happy that she was here. "I want to get lunch," she said in a miffed voice. "But if you're too busy for me ..." She pivoted and made a grab for the door knob. "Jesus!" She started as Quinn suddenly appeared behind her. Damn, Lycans were fast.

"Selena," he said in a warning voice. "What I meant was you should have waited for me at the library. It's not safe for you to be out on your own, especially around here. Someone could be watching the office."

"I'm here now and nothing happened. Take me to lunch," she demanded.

"I—" A beeping sound from the computer interrupted him, and he quickly walked back to his desk. He leaned down, brows furrowing as his eyes scanned the screen. "Shit!" Suddenly, his phone began to ring and vibrate, dancing across his desk as the device buzzed furiously. "Sorry, Selena, I gotta take this call."

She couldn't believe he was just ignoring her like that. He didn't even notice when she left and slammed the door.

"Selena, we need to talk," Evie said, blocking her way.

She tried to sidestep around the brunette, but Evie kept blocking her. "Fine. But I need wine with this conversation. I know where I want to go."

They walked to Muccino's Italian Restaurant, which was just

around the corner from Lone Wolf. Usually, Selena wouldn't splurge on such a place for lunch, but her bruised ego needed a bit of pampering today. The young hostess led them to a table in the corner and left them with a set of menus. Selena immediately asked for a glass of wine. Moments later, a waiter appeared with her drink and asked if they had decided on what to eat.

"Now," Evie began after their waiter had taken their orders. "What's going on, Selena? Connor came knocking at our door last night. He said someone tried to push you off the subway platform and that you'll be staying with Quinn from now on?"

"Well, that's about the gist of it," Selena said glumly, taking a sip of her wine. "Hmmm ... you don't suppose Chef McHottie is around, do you?" She glanced toward the kitchen doors, craning her neck for a sign of Dante Muccino, the restaurant's handsome head chef and part owner, who also happened to be a Lycan.

"Don't change the subject, Sel." Evie grabbed the wine glass. "Now, tell me. Are you sleeping with Quinn?"

Selena went bright red, all the way to the roots of her hair.

"Oh, no," Evie said, and she took a large swig from the wine glass.

"Hey, that's mine!" Selena grabbed the glass back. "You're buying me another one."

Evie's cheeks were flush from the alcohol. "You didn't! Since when?"

"Uh, since Merlin's?"

"That long? And you didn't tell me?" Evie pouted.

"Because I knew this is how you'd react! Ugh!" Selena finished off the wine. "Stop judging me. You're the one who kept going back to Dick even after he broke your heart and cheated on you multiple times."

"That's not the same thing," Evie retorted. "And I told you, I haven't talked to Richard since that last time. It's been months. I didn't even see him when I went back to Kansas."

"Good," Selena replied. "Because *Dick* was an asshole and you deserve better. Someone who will worship the ground you walk on and won't ever make you cry."

"Don't change the subject. So, you finally punched your v-card, huh?" Evie winked at her. "How was it?"

Selena looked at the empty glass of wine and raised it to the passing waiter. Then she turned to Evie. "Fan-fucking-tastic."

Evie laughed. "Oh my God. Quinn really did a number on you, huh?"

Selena sighed. "Well, you don't have to worry about that. I think Quinn's ready to move on to the next conquest." The bitterness in her voice was evident, and all she could think of was *where is that damned waiter with the wine?*

"Oh dear. I'm so sorry, Selena."

Ah, here he is. The waiter topped off her glass, and, when he stopped halfway, she flashed him a freezing look. The young man gulped and poured more wine.

"Go ahead, say it."

"Say what?"

"I told you so." Selena looked down at her wine.

"I'd never say that to you." Evie patted her hand. "Besides, how can you know that he's going to move on?"

"It's the only explanation," she said, taking a large sip. The wine was making her feel all warm and tingly now. "He only had sex with me once last night."

"Oh wow, only once," Evie said sarcastically, rolling her eyes. "Meanwhile, here I am, almost a year of no action."

"Jesus, Evie, if you want some action, I know another Lycan who could help with that." Selena hiccuped.

"Don't you dare!" Evie covered Selena's mouth with her hand.

Selena let out a muffled sound and shoved Evie's hand off her face. "You should try sex with a Lycan. It's *amazing*. Two words: supernatural refractory period."

"That's three words, Sel."

"Yeah, whatever. Tell me, when Connor knocked on the door last night, did he knock on anything else?"

"Selena, you're drunk." Evie took away her wine glass.

Selena giggled. "You li-ike him. You want to ki-iss him. And ma-a-rry him," she sing-songed.

"Shut up, Selena."

"Ladies."

Selena and Evie both gasped. A gorgeous man in a white chef's shirt was peering down at them, an amused look on his face.

"Chef McHottie!" Selena stood up, nearly falling back. Dante Muccino quickly snaked an arm around her waist to steady her. "Nice to see you again."

"Glad you came back, ladies," Dante said, then lowered his voice. "But would you mind keeping it down?"

Selena looked around and saw that the other diners were watching, many of them obviously annoyed.

"Oh shit," Selena said, slapping her hand over her mouth. She tended to get loud when she was tipsy. "Sorry, Chef."

He laughed, his mismatched blue and green eyes twinkling. "No worries. I know you're friends of the clan," he whispered close to her ear. "So you're welcome to stay, but, please, do remember there are also other people here."

"What the fuck is going on here?"

Selena blinked and then turned her head. "Quinn," she said with a sweet smile. "Nice of you to come out of your office."

Quinn's jaw was tight, and his arms were stiff at his sides. His eyes were blazing twin fires. "Get your hands off her," he said to Dante in a deadly voice. "Or I'll make you."

"Excuse me?" Dante let go of Selena and turned to Quinn, pushing up the sleeves of his chef's whites. "You don't tell me what to do in my restaurant, Lone Wolf."

Quinn stepped up and faced Dante. "Oh yeah? Well—"

"Quinn!" Selena hissed. "What are you doing here?"

"You walked out without telling me," Quinn replied, his eyes never leaving Dante's. "So I followed you here. Turns out, you didn't need me at all."

The air around her felt heavy with the two Lycans asserting their dominance over each other. Selena looked around them. Now everyone in the restaurant was really staring. "Quinn, quit it."

Quinn growled, but when Selena tugged at his arm, he relaxed. "Enjoy your lunch," he said, then turned to walk away.

Selena watched him leave. "Shit," she cursed and then chased after him, ignoring Evie's calls. She burst through the door and onto the sidewalk. He was already half a block away, and she had to run to catch up to him.

"Quinn!" She caught him by the arm. "Stop, Quinn! What is going on with you?"

He spun around, barely controlled anger masked his face. "What's going on with me? Why don't you tell me, huh? He had his damn hands all over you. I can still smell him on you."

She gasped. "Chef McHot—I mean, Chef Dante was at our table to tell us to tone it down. Then, clumsy me, I almost fell over and he caught me. I swear that's all it was."

Quinn grasped the sides of her face, and, for a moment, fear struck her when she saw the rage in his eyes. But he didn't do anything except rub his wrists down her neck. She inhaled his tantalizing aftershave, and the smell of freshly cut grass and sawdust seemed to stick to her skin. "Quinn ..."

He swooped down, catching her mouth in a rough kiss. His lips sought hers, devouring the softness, and she succumbed.

Wrapping her arm around his waist, she pressed up against him. "Why were you acting so weird today?"

"I'm sorry, kitten, I didn't mean to snap at you and ignore you. I just needed to work. I want to get this bastard, whoever he is. To keep you safe."

"I wish you had said something." She laid her head on his chest, listening to the beating of his heart. "I'm sorry about Dante. I was getting tipsy and clumsy."

"I can't stand anyone else touching you," he rasped. "I need you so bad."

"I'll call in sick," she whispered. "Let's go back to your place."

_____

$\mathcal{T}$he next couple days passed by without incident. That is, as long as a kitchen fire doesn't count as an incident. The night after Muccino's, Quinn was determined to show Selena he, too, could make fancy meals like Chef Dante. He ended up burning the steak, as well as his right hand when he tried to put out the fire. It seemed like Quinn's skills in the kitchen extended only to breakfast, so, like true New Yorkers, they called for delivery. That same night, they finally finished the last Lord of the Rings movie.

It became almost routine—Quinn took her to work first and picked her up, then they had dinner back at his place. Selena felt bad for leaving Evie alone, but Quinn assured her that her roommate was safe, especially if Connor was watching after her. Evie, on the other hand, didn't seem to know about her shadow, so Selena kept quiet. It was better if she didn't know anything more about the threats to Quinn's life. She didn't want to make her best friend panic.

Selena knew she should feel guilty, as her father was calling her at least once a day and had left her several voice messages. She hadn't even listened to them as she wanted to put off the decision. The truth was, there was no decision. Leonard had made himself very clear, even without saying the words: Marry Jason or leave the coven. But the only thing she felt guilty about was not telling Quinn. Every day, it was a looming thought in her head, and she couldn't stand lying to him. Because whatever was happening between them, it had gone way past a one-night stand. And if she didn't handle it now, it would surely explode in her face.

But what was she to do? She had a duty to her coven and her family. And she wanted children, eventually. She would love her children, no matter what, even if they didn't possess any power, but having some magic would surely shield them from the cruelty of other witches and warlocks.

She finally made a decision. When she was sure Quinn was safe, she would end things and accept Jason's proposal. The thought brought a stabbing pain to her chest, but she didn't have a choice. Quinn would never settle down with her anyway. He would tire of her eventually and then what? She would be the one left with her heart broken.

Her phone's ring tone jolted her out of her thoughts. Without thinking, she picked it up, hoping it might be Quinn, even though it was too early. He usually called her in the middle of the day just to say hello and sometimes tease her with dirty talk. He once gave her a searing description of how he was going to tie her up and make her come with his tongue as she was watching over a senior's book club.

"Isn't it a little early for your three o'clock?" she asked in a seductive voice.

"Selena, what are you talking about?"

She cringed. "Uh, hey Alexis." Her stepsister's voice was like a cold ocean wave, crashing over her and zapping all thoughts of sex out of her head. "What's up?"

"She's so weird," Alexis staged-whispered, probably to Katrina. "Selena, how are you?"

"I'm great." She swallowed a gulp. "Just great."

"So, I wanted to tell you, Katrina and I are coming to New York City," she said in her nasal voice that made Selena want to poke her eardrums out with a chopstick.

Selena bit back a retort. "Oh, that's nice."

"We were thinking, we should totally hang out at Merlin's," Alexis continued. "It's been ages since we've seen each other and Uncle Lucien."

Selena snorted inwardly. Uncle Lucien hated Alexis and Katrina almost as much as she did, as he saw through their fake facades. But why would they invite her to 'hang out?' Well, it was simple. They would never get through the door on their own. But if Selena were with them, Lucien would have no choice but to let them in. "I don't know, I'm kind of busy these days ..."

"Oh, that's too bad," Alexis said. "I was thinking you should bring your roommate, too. We were just over at your place, and we ran into her."

Shit.

"And I'm sure father would be thrilled to know you're not alone at home."

Double shit. Technically, even if she didn't possess any magic, Selena was supposed to declare to the coven if she lived with anyone. However, she didn't want the coven looking into Evie's background because if they found out about her mom being a Lycan, well, the elders would not like that and could force her to evict Evie.

"Actually, I'm free tonight," Selena said quickly. "Why don't we meet at Merlin's? Say, around eight p.m.?"

"Great," Alexis exclaimed. "We'll be there. See you at the door, Selena!"

As soon as Alexis hung up, Selena let out a groan. *Fuck my life.* She had a feeling Alexis and Katrina were going to cause a lot of trouble for her.

Crap, now she had to entertain her stepsisters. Maybe she could sneak them into Merlin's and then slip out before they noticed, then get back to Quinn's without him being any wiser. She bit her lip. She didn't want to lie to Quinn, but she also didn't want him to know where she was going and that her stepsisters were in town. If Alexis and Katrina even got a whiff of what was going on between her and Quinn ... she didn't even want to think about the consequences.

Her phone rang again, and she picked it up, relieved that it was Quinn this time. "Hey," she said in a small voice.

"Hey, kitten, are you being a good girl?"

She laughed. "I'm getting ready for Storytime. Of course, I'm a good girl."

He chuckled. "*Three Little Pigs* again?"

"No , *Little Red Riding Hood*."

He let out a dramatic sigh. "Don't you have stories where the wolf is the good guy?"

She laughed. "I'll try to find one next time." She bit her lip. *Here goes nothing.* "So, I was thinking, tonight ..."

Quinn let out an unhappy sound. "Yeah, about that. I'm sorry, I gotta work late tonight. Sebastian's put me on a case, and I'm dealing with this accident shit."

Jesus, Mary, and Joseph, hallelujah! "Oh, that's too bad." She tried to contain her relief.

"Yeah, I'm sorry. I'll bring you home, and then I gotta go right back to the office."

"Oh, no, don't worry about me," she insisted. "I can get home by myself. I have to go back to my apartment and pick up some clothes anyway."

"Will you be with Evie? I'd feel safe then because I know Connor's still tailing her."

"No. I mean, yes, I could be." An idea popped into her head. She took a deep breath, hoping he wouldn't freak out at her next statement. "You know, I haven't been much of a supportive friend to Evie. Her show premiered at Merlin's the other week, and I haven't seen it because you know ... we've been busy."

"Yeah," he laughed. "Very busy."

"Anyway, I was thinking of heading over there with her. To Merlin's. And there's no place safer. Uncle Lucien has some pretty strong magical protections around the entire building."

There was silence on the other end. "All right," he finally said. "I suppose you could have a girls' night out with Evie." His voice dipped low to a sexy rumble. "Just remember who's going to make you scream and moan after."

She gave a nervous laugh. "I will. Anyway, I have to get ready for Storytime."

"Fine. Make the wolf a little sympathetic this time, okay?"

"I'll try," she said wryly and then hung up.

Talk about great timing. This could work. She could get Alexis and Katrina in, get them a few drinks (she'd pay for them herself if that meant keeping them occupied) and then sneak out. Now, all she had to do was convince Evie to go with her, so it wouldn't technically be a lie.

Nothing could go wrong, could it?

Quinn stretched his arms over his head and let out a groan. It was already dark outside, and he was all alone in the Lone Wolf Security office. Killian had gone home long ago and Connor, as usual, didn't show up. Of course, he knew where Connor was—tailing Evie and Selena.

Normally, he'd be uneasy leaving Selena alone, but he had complete faith that his brother would keep both women safe if anything happened. Besides, as far as he knew, his troubles weren't connected to anything magical.

He let out a yawn. When had he eaten last? Hours ago, probably. But the good news was he was nearly done. Sebastian had been generous in letting him investigate the accident, but he wasn't paying them to figure out their own shit. Creed Security was having trouble with a client somewhere in East Africa. Quinn had been overconfident, thinking he could get into their servers quickly, but the place was apparently protected better than a penny in a miser's fist. He had to do it the old-fashioned way, which was to send a virus to someone on the inside. He checked his monitor and breathed a sigh of relief. One of his victims just opened the file. Now, the little program he embedded in the photo was working its magic, and soon he'd be able to find the right info on their servers.

A soft chime caught his attention, and he looked at his left monitor. There was a little red message icon in one of his private chat windows. He clicked on it.

I have the info you need.

Quinn bit his lip and then typed back: *What do you have?*

Information vital to your investigation. Send the payment to the usual account, and I'll forward it to you.

He retrieved his phone and logged onto the secure banking app for his Swiss bank account, then sent the payment over. This contact was expensive but had never let him down yet.

Payment received. Happy hunting.

Quinn immediately dragged the file from the chat window and clicked on it. It contained scans of reports and pictures. When he looked closer, he realized what it was.

"Sonafabitch!" He slammed his closed fists on the desk,

making the monitors rattle. The car wreck wasn't an accident. Worse than that, it was a cover up.

The first photo was that of the initial report, dated right after the incident. While the copy Quinn got indicated that it was an accident, this one said that the detective was unsure. The name of the detective on this report was different as well.

The next photo showed an autopsy photo of a half-burned body on a coroner's slab, along with an initial report. It was Jon Dover's body. The medical examiner had found a stab wound on his lower back, right into the kidney, which was the likely cause of death. The victim had bled out even before he burned in the crash. However, this was not the report filed with the NYPD, nor was this the same ME. Quinn paused to think. This meant Jon Dover was killed first and then his body placed in the car. Quinn thought for a moment. After that, it would have been easy enough to set the car to drive and crash it or hack into its electrical system and control it remotely.

Whoever did this was probably hoping the fire would disintegrate the body and destroy any evidence of murder. And when that didn't happen, they used other means—bribery or coercion —to cover up the findings.

So, he now had proof that the crash was no accident. If he had been trapped between the exploding car and the wall, even his Lycan healing abilities wouldn't have been able to save him. But who would want him dead? It had to be someone who had pull in the NYPD and Medical Examiner's office and probably had a lot of money or influence. Who the hell had he pissed off so much that he'd want him dead?

"Okay," he said aloud and then went back to his computer. Time to find out how the subway incident was connected. First, he would need to get camera footage and photos from around the subway station, anything from security cameras around the block to cell phone selfies from tourists. A quick message to his contact took care of that. Next, he needed a list of possible suspects from his past. That would be a long list, but he could narrow it down to people still active in the business. Finally, he needed a lead on the guy in the hoodie. Sebastian Creed had put him in touch with Alynna and Alex Westbrooke from the Alpha's office. He sent them an email, asking them for a list of male Lycans in the city and state who could match the description of hoodie guy—male, anywhere between eighteen to forty years old, and around six feet in height. There were only about 250 Lycans living in New York, so that should narrow it down.

He glanced at the clock again and gave a heavy sigh. Selena and Evie were probably at Merlin's. She had sent him a text about an hour ago when she reached her apartment and then again later when they were leaving. Grabbing his phone, he typed a message to Connor.

Are you at Merlins?

Outside was his brother's reply.

The girls?

Inside.

He rolled his eyes. Connor was as prolific with texting as he was in real life.

I'll be there in 10.

He didn't bother waiting for Connor's reply. After slipping his jacket on, he locked up the office and headed to Merlin's.

*I*t was easy enough to convince Evie to come with her to Merlin's. After all, she hadn't spent a lot of time with her best friend lately. They arrived at the club about fifteen minutes before she was supposed to meet Alexis and Katrina (which meant she actually had about forty-five minutes, since her stepsisters never showed up on time and loved making people wait). It gave her enough time to warn Uncle Lucien.

"You know, I could turn them away," the warlock said. "Then you wouldn't have to suffer their company. Correction, I wouldn't have to suffer their company."

Selena frowned. "Please, Uncle Lucien, just indulge them for now." If Alexis and Katrina didn't get their way, they'd make it *her* fault and then she'd be the one punished.

Lucien let out a long, suffering sigh. "Fine. You are my favorite niece after all. Someday, when you're ready to stand up for yourself, I'll have your back." He tipped up her chin. "My dear Selena, what would it take for you to believe you are worth a hundred of them?" His inky black eyes suddenly sparkled with mischief. "Or perhaps it's not a what, but a who?"

His words struck her deep. Selena wished her mother hadn't

died and her father had never remarried. Then she wouldn't have this problem. Or, if she had been born with even a smidgen of magic, then no one in her coven would give her those awful pitying looks. But if wishes were horses, then well … she would have a lot of horses. "I should go and see if they're here," Selena said glumly. "Thank you, Uncle Lucien."

"Of course, dear."

She had left Evie backstage. Her friend was talking to the dancers, making some last minute adjustments to the show so Selena went out to the front of the house. It was already starting to get packed. Obviously, the new, classier format of the show seemed to attract more people to the club. Merlin was still experimenting with the show, doing it only once a week and keeping the usual strip shows on other days. She made her way to the front of the house, waving to the two bouncers at the door. As soon as she got out, she immediately spotted her stepsisters.

"There you are," Alexis said in her grating voice.

"We've been waiting for ages," Katrina whined. Both of them were dressed up in skimpy outfits that showed off long legs and cleavage that left little to the imagination, plus enough makeup to cover a whole troupe of clowns.

"Sorry, I had to secure our table," Selena answered.

"Oh, did you get us a good one?" Alexis asked, flipping her long blond locks over one shoulder.

"Of course."

"Good." Katrina's eyes raked over her. "Ugh, you need to find better clothes, Selena."

Selena looked down at her little black dress, which she thought was sexy in an understated way. It certainly wasn't as flashy her stepsisters' outfits, but it was classy and didn't show off every bit of her skin. "It was the only clean thing I had," she said with a shrug.

"You should think about getting a Brazilian blowout to straighten that bird's nest you call hair," Alexis added.

Selena bit her lip to keep from making a retort about *their* hair extensions. "C'mon, let's go inside."

She led them inside to the table Uncle Lucien had reserved for them—up front, one of the best in the house.

"Ugh, did Uncle Lucien stick us in the loser's section?" Katrina sneered as she looked around them.

Selena curled her hands into fists under the table. "Katrina," she said in an even voice. "We're right in front with no obstructions. And Uncle Lucien gave us this table without the usual fee."

Alexis laughed. "Well, he should. We are his nieces."

"I'm his niece," Selena muttered under her breath.

"Why are we up here with these old farts?" Katrina whined.

"These 'old farts' are Merlin's best customers and came all the way here to watch the new show," Selena said in an exasperated tone. The witches and warlocks around them were not old at all, but definitely more established. They were the ones who had the money to be able to afford a table.

"Yeah, well, who cares about the show?" Alexis said. "I'm only here for the alcohol."

Katrina eyed a passing waiter who was shirtless and had a well-toned chest. "Oh, do you think we can get to the VIP room in the back?"

"I'm sure Selena could manage that, right?" Alexis winked at her.

"I'll see what I can do." Selena groaned inwardly. Why was she such a pushover when it came to Katrina and Alexis? Maybe because they could make her life miserable, as they had almost all her life. They somehow had the power to manipulate everyone around them to make them appear the victims and Selena the oppressor. She had learned over the years it was better to let them have their way, rather than face their wrath.

As they were waiting for the show to begin, Katrina and Alexis chatted about gossip from the coven and whatever spell they were working on that week. Selena knew they did this on purpose—not only to rub her nose in the fact that she didn't have any power, but also that she wasn't in the coven's inner circle. Normally, their conversation would make her feel bad about her lack of talent, but, tonight, all she felt was impatience.

Checking her watch, she tapped it, wondering if it was running slow. She could bring Katrina and Alexis to the VIP room backstage where Uncle Lucien had set up a meet-and-greet of sorts for his best clients. It was a chance to mingle with the performers, plus there was a spread of champagne and hors d'oeuvres. She'd hand them some bubbly and then slip out and get back to the loft, maybe even before Quinn got home, if she was lucky.

***

*B*y the time Quinn reached Merlin's, there was no line outside and the main door was shut. Connor was standing outside, leaning against the brick wall.

"Are they not letting anyone in or is it just us?" Quinn asked.

"Full capacity. Plus, they didn't want anyone interrupting the show once it started." Connor's tone was acrid, though his face remained stony.

"The girls are in there?"

He nodded. "They arrived before the show started, then Selena came out for a while and went back in with two blondes."

"Women?"

"Witches, probably."

Selena didn't mention meeting any other friends. *Strange.* Although, Merlin's was a witch hang out, so it would make sense if she bumped into some friends.

"Are we gonna wait out here all night?"

Quinn shook his head. "Nah, let's go in and say hi to the girls."

"No way we're going to get in there," Connor pointed out. "Not after last time."

"Who said we were going to go through the front door? C'mon." Quinn gestured to the back of the building. "I know how we can get in."

They walked to the rear of the building to a dark alley. At first glance, it didn't seem like it was part of the club, but that was probably because of the magical protections around it. However, since Quinn had already been here, the spell didn't work on him.

"Are you sure we're in the right place?"

"Yeah, this is where all the dancers take their smoke break. Daric showed me this exit. Said it might be useful one day to know it." Quinn didn't realize it would be handy tonight. He supposed he should have gone back to the loft and waited for Selena to come home, but something felt off. Like Selena was hiding something from him. The feeling just didn't sit right with him. Even Wolf was pacing, urging him to see her and make sure everything was okay.

They walked down the darkened alley as a strange sensation crawled over his skin, reminding Quinn of their last battle with the mages in Norway. It was probably the magic spells all around them. Even Connor seemed more on edge than usual. But he pressed on, knowing what was at the end. There was a metal door, which, much to his relief, was unlocked. They entered and soon found themselves inside the backstage area of Merlin's.

"Now what?"

"We go check on the girls, and then maybe Selena and I can finally go home, and I can put this day behind me." He hadn't told anyone about what he had discovered. Tomorrow, he would tell Connor and Killian, but tonight, all he wanted was to hold Selena in bed and lose himself in her.

Quinn had only spent one night as an entertainer in Merlin's, but the backstage area was small enough that he didn't get lost. Hmmmm ... where to begin searching? Quinn frowned. There were way too many attractive men back here. Attractive and half-naked men, he thought as two dancers wearing nothing but red Speedos passed by them in the hallway. Why the hell he agreed to let Selena come here in the first place, he didn't know. Well, actually, he did know. Lucien Merlin was her family, after all, so it wasn't like he could object to her spending time here. He wasn't some controlling asshole boyfriend.

"Where the hell are they?"

A familiar feminine laugh approaching them answered Connor's question. It wasn't Selena though, but Evie. And she wasn't alone.

"Jack, you were awesome," Evie said to her companion.

"Well, I had a great director and choreographer," Jack replied, nudging her with his shoulder. He was wearing the same costume Quinn had seen him in during the rehearsal—black briefs, top hat, and leather boots, but his sparkly red jacket was slung over his shoulder.

"I like that extra move you did at the end with the—Quinn? Connor?" Evie's eyes went wide as saucers as her gaze landed on them. "What are you guys doing here? I thought Selena said you were working late."

Quinn felt the air thicken around them, and he sent Connor a warning look. Not that his brother paid him any mind as he continued to glare at Evie and Jack. "I finished up early. Where is she?"

"She's probably in the VIP room with Lucien and her step-sisters," Evie said.

"Her what?" Selena never mentioned she had stepsisters or that they were coming tonight. Did Selena keep this from him? Were they the reason she thought to come here? That feeling that didn't sit right with him? It was suddenly growing.

"I'm gonna go say hi then." Quinn straightened his shoulders and walked toward the VIP room, leaving Evie to deal with Connor.

20

*S*elena rolled her eyes as Katrina and Alexis giggled at the two strippers—er, entertainers—who were flirting with them. Of course, when they announced themselves as the boss's "favorite nieces," many of the guys were quick to fawn over them. They also positioned themselves strategically, ensuring that Selena was right behind them, blocked off from any of the males. Her stepsisters were taller than her, so she couldn't even see the rest of the room, and, thus, was trapped between their stick-thin bodies and the refreshment table and delegated to pouring them champagne whenever they waved their empty glasses at her.

Not that she minded. Selena didn't care for these nitwits. Even if they were hot, the fact that they could easily fall for Katrina and Alexis' charm made them so *not* hot in her eyes. Besides, she already had a sexy man waiting for her in bed. A smile curved on her lips, thinking of Quinn. He easily outshone all these guys in the looks department alone. If anything, she was more annoyed that she couldn't get out *right now*. Hopefully, they would move out of her way so she could sneak out. But it was like they were torturing her. Double torturing her because not only did she have to suffer their company (and get whipped in the face by blond hair extensions every couple seconds), but also because she couldn't get to the delicious Lycan waiting to do naughty things to her in bed.

"Katrina, Alexis, why don't you give poor Selena a chance to breathe?" Uncle Lucien's cool voice interrupted the loud chatter from the two. "And perhaps leave some champagne for my other, *paying* guests?"

"Oh, Uncle Lucien, such a kidder!" Alexis brayed. She stepped aside. Katrina snorted beside her. "Sorry, Selena. I didn't notice you were there."

"Yeah, whatev," Selena muttered as she pushed her way out of their circle. She took a deep breath, finally free of the oppressive cloud of perfume that followed her stepsisters. "Thanks," she said to Lucien gratefully.

He smiled at her. "Don't thank me yet, my dear. I think trouble has just begun." Lucien nodded to the entrance of the VIP room.

"Oh shit."

Quinn was standing there, his brows furrowed and his eyes scanning the room. Selena's heart slammed against her ribcage, and, for a moment, she wanted to duck and run. Or hide. Then, as if the karmic gods heard her and decided to pay her back for every single bad thing she did throughout her entire life, Quinn's gaze crashed on her.

"Crap." So much for her escape plan.

As soon as he saw her, he strode over, quickly reaching where she and Lucien stood. "Merlin." He nodded to Lucien. "Nice spread."

"Lycan. I don't remember inviting you here," Lucien replied, but his tone was more amused than mad. Like he had been expecting Quinn all this time. "I should go, Selena dear. I'll see you around." He gave Quinn a raised brow and then walked away.

"What are you doing here?" she asked in a quiet whisper.

"I finished work early, so I wanted to see you. Why are you whispering?"

She gave a nervous laugh. "Whispering? Was I whispering?"

He crossed his arms over his chest. "What is going on, Selena?"

"Going on?" she echoed. "I told you, I'm here to see the show. And support Evie." She glanced around. Where was her best friend?

"She's outside," Quinn said as if reading her mind.

"Right. Well, thanks for coming. Let's go home." She grabbed his hand and tugged him toward the door.

"Selena, who's your friend?"

She dropped Quinn's hand like it was a piece of hot coal. "Motherfucker," she muttered. She pasted a smile on her face. "Alexis. Katrina." She swallowed audibly. "This is Quinn. Quinn, these are my stepsisters."

Alexis' eyes devoured Quinn. "Oh my," she giggled. "Selena never told us she had such a charming ... friend."

Katrina's nostrils flared. "A charming *Lycan* friend."

Quinn frowned. "Hmmm ... that's odd. She never mentioned you guys either."

"How silly of her," Alexis said with a chuckle. "But then she's always so absentminded and forgetful. Oh my," she said, running her hands down Quinn's bicep. "Do you work out?"

"I'm sure he's naturally *talented*," Katrina added, sidling up to his other side. "He's a Lycan, after all. Is it true what they say about your kind?"

Quinn laughed. "Exactly what have you been hearing?"

"Oh look," Selena said weakly. "I think they refilled the hors d'oeuvres table." She walked away from the trio, unable to bear hearing her sisters fawn over Quinn and him basking in their attention.

This was it. This was what she had been dreading. But she never thought Quinn would fall for her sisters' siren call. It was doubly excruciating, and she washed down the bitter lump in her throat with half a glass of champagne.

"Selena, there you are!" Evie said, appearing behind her. "What are they doing here?"

"Who?"

The brunette nodded to the other side of the room at Quinn and her sisters. Connor joined them as well. "Quinn and Connor. How did they get ... hey, are those your sisters? They were waiting outside our apartment today."

"Stepsisters," she glumly corrected. It was like a train wreck, and she couldn't look away. Alexis had obviously staked her claim on Quinn, while Katrina was trying to cozy up to Connor, much to the other Lycan's consternation.

"What are they doing?" Evie said, grabbing Selena's arm. Her fingernails dug into her skin.

"Ow, hey, watch it!"

Evie's face was redder than a tomato, and her eyes were throwing daggers at Katrina. Despite herself, Selena suppressed a grin. "Cool it, Evie. He's in no way interested in her. In fact, he looks really uncomfortable right now." Katrina started running her hands up and down Connor's bicep, giving it a playful squeeze. Connor stood there, his back as stiff as a board, his brows furrowing.

"I don't know what you mean."

Selena gave a mental eye roll. Evie was a smart girl, but, sometimes, she could be so dumb. Or pretended to be.

"*Now* what are they doing?"

Quinn put an arm around both girls and then said something to Connor. Both Lycans walked toward the door with the girls.

Tears burned at Selena's eyes, but she refused to let them fall. She grabbed a mini tart from the table and swallowed it whole, the pastry tasting like ash in her mouth.

"Well, I don't give a flying fuck about him—them—at all," Evie said as if agreeing with her. "He can have her and her magical tits and sparkly pussy." She took a champagne flute from the table and downed it one gulp. "I—Selena, are you okay?"

"Me?" She gave a tight laugh. "Of course I'm fine. Perfectly fine."

Evie looked at the door where the foursome had disappeared and back to Selena. "Oh my god. Selena, are you in l—"

"Sorry, I have to go to the bathroom," Selena mumbled, as she walked away from Evie. The humiliated, deflated feeling began to creep into her, and she just prayed she'd make it outside before she broke down. She walked out of the VIP room, her hurried steps leading her toward the private exit Uncle Lucien had shown her before.

"Selena! Selena, wait up!"

She stiffened, hearing Quinn's voice. She took a deep breath and wiped away the tears that had gathered in her eyes with the back of her hand. "Yes?" she asked brightly, turning to face him. She would not let him see how hurt she was.

"Oh good, you're ready to go," Quinn said. "C'mon, I'm starving and tired. We can order in tonight."

Her brows knitted in confusion. "What? I mean, what about Alexis?"

"Huh?" He looked at her as if she were crazy. "Your stepsister?" He shuddered. "God, I thought I was never getting away from her. Now I know what women mean when they say they feel like a piece of meat. I think I'm going to need a shower as soon as we get home. That perfume she's wearing is sticking to my shirt."

Shock struck her system like lightning. "But ... you left with them."

Quinn chuckled. "Yeah, I had to get them out of there. Connor's stuck with them now," he said gleefully. "I think I'm just about done getting Connor back for kicking my ass."

Selena couldn't suppress her laugh, thinking of Connor and her stepsisters. She felt a twinge of guilt. Connor wasn't a bad guy, so she didn't agree that the punishment fit the crime in this instance.

Quinn let out a sigh. "Why didn't you tell me about your stepsisters? Or that they were in town? Are they the real reason you're here?"

Selena bit her lip. She didn't want to lie to Quinn. "Yes. I'm sorry. I just ... I don't know how to explain our relationship. Not just to you, but to anyone."

"Is it the power thing? With your coven?"

She nodded.

"You don't have to explain things to me, Selena." He drew her into his arms. "And I know I haven't been that open with you, so I'm not one to give you a lecture. Now, let's go home."

She stiffened in his arms and then pulled back to look up at him. Quinn didn't want her stepsisters. Quinn chose her. He chose to be with her. Warmth spread over her, and she forgot the momentary hurt she felt. "Yes, let's go home."

Selena lay in the big bed, Quinn's arm over her waist. He had been asleep for a while, but she couldn't quiet her mind long enough to drift off. That pit in her stomach was forming again. It was like a bad feeling she couldn't shake.

They went straight home from Merlin's, not bothering to say goodbye to Uncle Lucien, Evie, or even Connor. She sent a quick apology text to her friend and then turned her phone off. All she wanted was to be alone with Quinn. As soon as they were, he swept her up into his arms and made love to her. He was gentle and sweet tonight, taking his time with her. As they both approached their orgasms, he gazed right into her face, his eyes like twin blue fires boring into her soul. It scared her and excited her at the same time. She felt out of control and like she was hurtling into some unknown she wouldn't be able to recover from. When she fell apart, she raked her nails down his back and screamed his name. Tears streamed down her cheeks, and she quickly wiped them away before he saw them.

Selena felt lost. She never expected this, never asked for this. All she wanted was to lead a quiet life and be truly accepted by her people. If she was really honest with herself, she had thought if she had a magically talented child, the coven would stop feeling for her and finally respect her. But she knew now that would not only be incredibly selfish, but also unfair to Jason and any child of hers.

"Can't sleep?" Quinn murmured against her neck.

"I have a lot on my mind."

"Care to talk about it?"

She shook her head.

Quinn let out a sigh. "C'mon, maybe some hot milk will help you sleep." He got up and rolled off the bed, pulling on his boxers. Selena followed, grabbing her robe from the foot of the bed, then padding down to the kitchen with him.

She sat on one of the stools around the kitchen island and watched him take some milk out of the fridge and put it in a pan. "You look like you know what you're doing," she said in an amused voice.

"Archie used to do this for me when I couldn't sleep. I would stay up until all hours of the night, tinkering on my computer, and he'd come into my room at three a.m., begging me to get some rest. He would bribe me with warm milk. Eventually, I did get some sleep." He let the pot warm up on the stove, then poured the milk into a mug for her.

"Do you miss him?"

"Every day," Quinn said with a sad smile as he handed her the mug.

"You should be glad for the time you got to spend with him."

"I am," he said with a shrug. "I'm grateful for everything he gave me."

Selena took a sip of the warm liquid. "How did he find you?"

Quinn paused, but before she could say anything else, he started talking. "I would hang out at this warehouse with a bunch of other kids. Troublemakers, all of us." He gave a small laugh. "We were messing around with computers, trying to see what kind of trouble we could get in. At the end of the day, though, all those other kids went back to their homes with their parents. Not me. I lived in that warehouse. I ran away from ..." He paused and swallowed, but continued. "I learned how to hack ATMs for money, and I'd been on my own for a few years then. I was fourteen."

She gasped. That was so young. Too young to be without any parents and on his own. "Then what happened?"

"Archie came to this warehouse and scared the other kids away. Told them he was from the FBI and he was going to call all their parents. They all left except me, of course. I didn't have anywhere else to go. So he introduced himself to me. Told me the truth and that he knew what I was. Actually, I was so scared, Wolf came out."

"Wolf?"

"Yeah, that's what I call him. My animal. Not at first, though. It was tough being a Lycan during puberty and not having any help. I couldn't control it, and I'd just shift at random times and sometimes I wasn't sure when I'd change back. Archie helped. That first time, he wasn't scared of Wolf. He was able to make Wolf calm down enough to let me get back my body. Archie told me that I had to learn to control my animal. I'd been without help for too long, it seemed almost like an alien parasite living in my body. Archie said it might help if I treated it like it was a friend. So I started doing that."

"Did it help?"

"Yeah, though sometimes you'd think Wolf is in charge." A low rumbling came from his chest, and he laughed.

She smiled and then put the mug down. She walked around the island over to his side and then wrapped her arms around his waist, snuggling against his back. This man ... who knew she would ever meet such a person? She clung to him tighter. She had to tell him. No, not at this moment. First, she had to decline Jason's offer. The guilt of keeping the arrangement from Quinn weighed her down, keeping her awake. Jason would probably understand. She'd tell him it just didn't feel right. Her father ... well, that was an entirely different conversation, and she would have to take things one at a time.

"Feeling sleepy now?"

She nodded. Yes, that was it. Time to come clean to Quinn and finally she could move on with her life. She yawned and closed her eyes, letting Quinn lift her up and carry her back to the bedroom.

21

"You're sure about this?" Killian said, his face serious.

"Yes. My sources are never wrong. And you've read these reports yourself."

Killian let out a low whistle. "Shit, Quinn, who the hell did you piss off that would want you dead?"

"Who the hell wouldn't want me dead? You know the type of work we were in. We always knew we would be in danger."

Connor shifted in his seat uncomfortably. "Yeah, well, that's why Archie taught us to be careful."

"Any leads on the guy on the subway platform?" Killian asked.

"I'm working on it now. I have about a hundred or so names of adult male Lycans in New York to sift through. Then, once I narrow them down to those who fit the description, I can start looking at alibis."

"Good. Let me know when you have the names and we can split up the work." Killian took a folder from under his desk. "Now, we need to discuss Lone Wolf business, but, Quinn, finding this guy is your priority. I'll take care of Creed."

Quinn nodded. He was glad his brothers had his back. After all, he had no one else in the world after Archie died and his birth father all but sent him away. A small voice suddenly told him there was one more person. A small smile tugged at the corner of his mouth as he thought about Selena last night. How she could possibly think he would choose those airhead sisters of hers was beyond him. Okay, so once upon a time, he was shallow enough to have gone after them or girls like them. But who the hell would want chuck steak when they had grade A filet mignon at home? He licked his lips, thinking of how he was going to feast on Selena tonight. He quickly glanced at the clock on his phone. He was counting down the hours until he was out of here.

The rest of the afternoon passed by quickly enough, especially with the amount of work he had to do. By five p.m., he had only whittled his list down to half. New York was one of the biggest Lycan clans in the world. But shifters were loyal to their Alpha and clan and, with their dwindling numbers, few would dare kill another of their kind. Whoever was out to get him was powerful and had loyal people under his command. His thoughts strayed to Grant Anderson, but he dismissed that. The Alpha of New York would never attempt to cover up a murder. As the leader of the clan and the territory, he could kill Quinn himself if he had reason to and no one would even bat an eyelash.

His brain fried from work, Quinn decided to call it a day and walked down to the parking garage. He was always on his guard, and he took every precaution. He drove Selena and himself to work every day, even if they could easily walk or cab it. Before he even opened the door to his vehicle, he used a portable electronic scanner over the entire car to ensure no one had tampered with it or attached a bomb or a tracking device. He also locked down the onboard computer and added his own security features. No one would mess with his ride, especially not when he and Selena were in it.

The drive to the library was quick, and he was lucky enough to find a parking spot right in front. Quinn put the car into park and cut the engine.

As he was walking to the front door, he let out a groan. Alexis and Katrina were outside the library. They saw him and locked eyes, so it was too late to walk away or hide.

"Quinn," Alexis said in that voice that made Quinn's ears bleed. "What happened to you last night? I thought you were going to show us the private rooms at Merlin's?"

"An emergency came up. With my ... sister. But Connor was with you, right?"

Katrina pouted. "Your brother may be hot, but he's rude as fuck. He shoved us into the VIP room and then closed the door behind us."

Quinn tried not to laugh. "Oh, maybe he had an emergency, too."

"What are you doing here?" Alexis said, her painted-on eyebrow rising up to her hairline.

"I was ... uh ..." Shit, he and Selena never talked about what they would tell everyone. He supposed he was her boyfriend now, a realization that smacked him in the face. He never thought he'd be a one-woman man, but here he was, about to pick up his girlfriend from work and bring her home. He was so whipped, and he had never been happier. "I was going to drive Selena home," he said, which technically wasn't a lie. His heart raced, thinking about Selena in his home. No, their home. He'd ask her to move in tonight. The thought of being away from her for another minute made his chest ache. Wolf was getting impatient too, wanting these bitches to get out of the way.

Katrina and Alexis looked at each other, then they gave him twin smiles.

"Oh, you're an awfully nice *friend*," Alexis said. "I'm sure Jason would appreciate a friend like you taking care of Selena."

"Who?"

"Jason Ward," Katrina tittered. "You know, Selena's fiancé."

"What the fuck did you just say?" Quinn snarled. Because surely she didn't just say 'fiancé.'

Alexis gave Quinn a smug smile. "Doesn't Selena talk about him? The engagement party's next week, so she must have mentioned it to you."

"No. She did not." Quinn stood very still, and blood roared in his ears.

"They've been friends since childhood," Katrina added. "It's quite sweet, isn't it, Alexis? Childhood best friends turned sweethearts and soon to be man and wife."

"Really sweet." Alexis' eyes glinted. "Don't you think so, Quinn?"

"I should go see if Selena's ready," he said through gritted teeth. His mind was reeling as he walked through the doors of the library. He would get to the bottom of this.

*S*elena stretched her arms over her head, pushing the last book from the trolley onto the top shelf. "Finally." She breathed aloud as the book slipped into position without any problem. She brushed her palms together, mentally patting herself for a job well done. Having spent most of the afternoon putting books back into circulation and straightening up the shelves, she felt like she had walked miles today. But she was all done now. The library was also empty, which meant she could close up as soon as she clocked out.

Checking her watch, she saw it was five minutes past the hour. Quinn was probably out by her desk, already waiting for her. Her heart fluttered, thinking of him. At the same time, that pit in her stomach was getting bigger. For some reason, her father stopped calling and leaving her messages. She thought she was free, but a cryptic text from him this morning made the pit grow into the size of the Grand Canyon.

Stop ignoring me. If you don't decide, I'll do it for you.

It sent a chill straight to her bones but also cemented her decision. It was time she grew up. If she didn't fight for herself, then no one would.

Selena had already bought her train tickets to Philadelphia for the next day to turn down Jason's proposal. She would do it in person, of course. This was not a conversation to be done over text. Tonight though, she would tell Quinn. She had been practicing her speech the whole day. First, she would explain that this was how things were done in their society. Next, she would show him the tickets and tell him she was determined to do this. She prepared herself for the worst, in case he got mad about the whole marriage proposal thing, but surely he would understand. She and Jason hardly knew each other and hadn't even kissed or held hands. It was only Quinn. She was choosing him over her own family and her coven. It was risky, but she believed Quinn would see reason, especially since she was coming clean.

"Selena."

She nearly jumped out of her skin when she heard his voice. "Jesus, Quinn, you scared me," she said with a laugh, pressing her hand on her chest to calm herself. Hmmm...he had this brooding expression on his face that made him seem oh-so-sexy. As far as she knew, there should be no one else around. What if...

"Come closer, tiger," she purred. Oh wow. Did she really say that? Could she possibly...

Quinn moved closer, the blue of his eyes almost glowing. It

made her skittish and nervous, but, also excited. He placed two hands on her shoulders and backed her up against the wall between the stacks.

"You really must be a witch," he whispered in an oddly cool voice. "Because you've cast some sort of spell on me that no matter how many times I fuck you, I can't get enough." A rough hand moved up between her legs and fingers yanked her lace panties aside as he pushed them into her.

She gasped and grabbed at his shoulders to steady herself. "Yes, Quinn...don't stop." This really was happening. A zing of excitement raced through her body. "Quinn!" she shuddered, her body convulsing with pleasure. Her orgasm wasn't even done when he twisted her around, pressing her against the cold concrete.

"Did you like that, kitten?" His smile didn't reach his eyes.

"Yes," she moaned. "Please."

"Please what, Selena? Tell me what you want."

"I want you. Here. Now."

"Beg me for it."

"Take me, Quinn. Fuck me now."

He let out a cold laugh. "Tell me, Selena. Would you beg Jason Ward for it?"

Her eyes flew open and she looked up at him. The blue of his eyes was hard and emotionless, sending chills down the back of her legs. Selena's heart dropped all the way down to her stomach, and she swallowed loudly. She opened her mouth to speak, but nothing came out.

His mouth spread into a thin-lipped smile. "Well? Were you going to tell me?"

"How did you know?" she managed to say. Oh God. Her father. His message to her this morning. This was what he was trying to say. He probably found out about Quinn.

"Does it matter? You're not denying it, so it must be true."

"Quinn, you don't understand—"

"I don't understand?" he said, his voice rising. "All this time … you were fucking me and you had a fiancé."

A fist wrapped around her heart and Selena couldn't breathe. No, this wasn't the plan. She was going to come clean to him and explain. She could still explain. "I don't. I mean, it's not what you think. I haven't told him—"

"Then tell me what I'm supposed to think? You jump into bed with me, and this entire time you had another guy waiting in the wings?" The anger rolling off him was palpable now. "Well, at least I popped your cherry," he whispered into her ear, his breath hot. "Hope he doesn't mind that a Lycan got to your pretty little snatch first."

Quinn's cruel words sliced into her, and her knees buckled. Large hands propped her up and held her against the wall. "What do you say, Selena? One last fuck before you walk down the aisle?"

Asshole. Why wouldn't he let her explain? "Let go of me," she said weakly, her resolve weakening as Quinn's warm hands inched up her ribcage to cup her breasts.

"I can smell you. You want me." He nuzzled her neck, eliciting a whimper from her throat.

This was all her fault. If only she'd told him about Jason right away. But Leonard got to him somehow.

"Fuck, Selena, I can't believe how much I want you still … even though you're a liar," he growled.

"No!" She wrenched away from him, grabbing the shelves for support as she forced her legs to put as much space between them as she could.

"Why, Selena?" he asked in an anguished voice.

She took a deep breath and turned around. Quinn stood there, his face tight with strain. Why didn't she tell him? Because she was a fucking coward, that's why. Scared of her feelings for him and scared of his reaction. She was hedging her bets, trying to be sure and wanting to have her cake and eat it, too. Now was the time for honesty, even if it was too late. "Because I didn't want to fall in love with you. Not when I knew I couldn't keep you forever. It would have destroyed me to see you move on to the next pretty thing that caught your eye when you got tired of me."

"That's bullshit."

"Is it, Quinn?" she challenged. "You didn't want anything more than a quick lay from me. Have you honestly not tried to fuck other girls since you slept with me?"

Her question was met with silence. "You should have told me."

"Yes, yes, I know," she shot back. "And I'm sorry. I made a mistake in not telling you. I wish I could turn back time and do it all over again, but I can't."

His jaw ticked, and his eyes burned bright blue. "Shit ... I can't be here ... not now ..." He whipped around savagely and tore down the stacks like he was on fire, disappearing from her view.

Tears burned at her eyes, and the sob stuck in her throat escaped, a guttural sound ripping from her mouth. She should have listened to her instincts and stayed away from him. Her brain screamed at her. Loving Quinn would only lead to hurt, and, now, all she wanted to do was rip out her heart so she wouldn't feel the pain anymore.

She walked back to her desk, so ready to leave and go home so she could drown her sorrows in a bottle of wine or a carton of ice cream. She had left her phone on her desk, and it started ringing the moment she got back, which only made her want to throw it across the room. When she saw her father's name flash on the screen, she picked it up impulsively.

"What do you want?"

"Selena," Leonard answered. "Are you ready to give me your answer now?"

"What did you do?" she accused. How did he get to Quinn?

He snorted. "I didn't do anything, but you might as well know I've made it clear to the Wards and Jason that your answer will be the one they're hoping for. And that there are no other impediments to your marriage."

"Are you crazy?" she roared into the phone, her anger boiling over. "I'm never marrying him. Never!"

"Selena, you will do as I say or suffer the consequences."

"You wouldn't dare."

"Try me," Leonard challenged. "You'll never step foot in Philadelphia again. The coven will shun you and you'll never visit your mother's grave."

She already lost Quinn. What else could she lose now? "All right," she answered, swallowing the lump in her throat. "Fine. I mean, yes."

"Good. I'll send you a message with all the details of the engagement party."

22

*Q*uinn shut his eyes, hoping the reds and pinks streaking across the sky outside his bedroom were just a figment of his imagination. But they weren't. It was another morning in his miserable life. He let out a groan and rolled over in bed, wrapping himself around a pillow.

Sleep eluded him for the past couple days, and when he did finally crash out of pure exhaustion, he never got more than a couple hours of sleep. He spent every waking moment he had thinking about that day in the library and of Selena's betrayal. He thought being rejected by his father was the worst pain he'd ever felt, but he was wrong.

It was all too much, finding out about her engagement after all they had shared. Wolf was threatening to rip out from his skin. His control was slipping, and there was nowhere safe for him to shift in the library, so he had done the only thing he could do. He called his brother-in-law, Daric, for help. The warlock had the power to take him away from there, and he came just in time. Daric whisked him away to some forest in the middle of nowhere where he could let Wolf take over. The animal ran and ran for miles, it seemed, until it was exhausted.

Hours later, Daric found him lying under a bush. He was in human form, his body healing from various scratches. Quinn made Daric promise not to tell anyone. His brother-in-law said he would not lie to his siblings, especially Meredith, but would not offer the information either. Quinn hoped Meredith wouldn't suspect anything.

The loud banging on the door and the insistent ringing of the doorbell woke him up hours later. Quinn put a pillow over his head and hoped whoever it was would go away. After a few minutes, the noise stopped.

"Get up," Meredith said in an annoyed voice as she ripped the pillow from his head.

So much for Meredith not finding out. "What are you doing in here?" he groaned. "Did you break into my apartment?"

"Well, what was I supposed to do?" she asked

"How about *not* break into my apartment?"

"You weren't answering the door," she pointed out. Quinn opened his eyes and gave Meredith an angry stare. His sister looked right back at him, hands on her hips, her pregnant belly sticking out of her middle. She was wearing a shirt that read, 'We're hoping it's a unicorn.'

"What the hell is going on with you, Quinn?" Meredith dragged the sheet from his body. "Eww. When was the last time you showered?"

"Take a hike, Mer," Quinn muttered, rolling away from his sister.

"You smell, and this place is a mess." She motioned around his bedroom, which was littered with empty takeout containers and boxes. "Why are you living like this? And why haven't you come to work in days?"

Quinn let out a growl. "How the hell did you know that?"

"Killian asked me to come in and help out with some projects. Things you're supposed to be doing," Meredith pointed out. "Then, he tells me you haven't been to work in a week. It also looks like you haven't left your apartment or taken a shower or even slept in that time." She sat down gingerly next to him. "Now tell me what's going on."

"If I take a shower, will you leave me alone?"

She crossed her arms over her chest. "It's a start. Now go before your stench makes me puke all over your dirty sheets."

Quinn grumbled, but obeyed, lumbering towards the bathroom. What was it about Meredith that no one could say no to her?

He breathed a sigh as the hot water sprayed all over his greasy hair and skin. It felt good, he had to admit. He scrubbed himself, washing his hair and skin with some shampoo and body wash. Running a hand over his face, he supposed he also needed a shave, but it would take too long. He had to make Meredith leave now. He finished showering and stepped out of the stall.

"Wear this," Meredith said as she stormed into the bathroom, holding a pile of neatly folded clothes.

"What the fuck, Meredith?" Quinn said as he covered his crotch with his hands.

"Wear these outside clothes. You'll feel better when you're not in your underwear all the time."

"Fine," he groused, ripping a towel from the rack. "Now get the fuck out of my bathroom."

As Quinn dried himself off, he wiped the fog from his mirror and stared at his reflection. "Jesus." No wonder Meredith was pissed. He looked like shit. His facial hair was scraggly, he needed a haircut, and the dark smudges under his eyes weren't bags as much as they were an entire collection of luggage.

Turning away from his reflection, he finished dressing and padded out to his bedroom. The empty boxes of food were gone, and Meredith was stripping the bed. "You should burn these," she said holding one of the sheets away from her body.

"Whatever," he answered. "What will it take for you to leave?"

Meredith walked up to him and crossed her arms. She was three or four inches shorter than him, but she looked him straight in the eye. "The only way I'm leaving here is with you. I'm going to make you come to work today."

"Oh yeah? You and what army?"

"I don't need an army," she replied. "I have a warlock, and your boss is a literal fire-breathing dragon. Or do you want to tell Sebastian yourself why you haven't been to work?"

"You wouldn't."

"Try me."

Quinn let out a frustrated sound. "Fine. Let's go and get this over with." If he needed to work to get Meredith off his back, then that was what he was going to do. Besides, maybe this was what he needed to get his mind off Selena.

Meredith gave him a sweet smile. "Good."

As they walked out of the loft, they passed by the living room. Quinn ignored the claw and teeth marks that marred the leather couch and wooden coffee table. Meredith raised an eyebrow at him but didn't say anything.

Outside, the air was clean and crisp. Though he grumbled the entire time, Quinn was somewhat grateful to be outside. Even Wolf perked up a bit. The damn animal went from fighting with him to ignoring him. It stopped making its presence known in the last day or so, and Quinn was starting to get worried. Was Wolf broken beyond repair? Was *he*?

When they arrived at the Lone Wolf Security office, Killian and Connor were already waiting at the reception area.

"What the hell is this?" Quinn looked at each of his siblings. "A fucking intervention?"

"What's going on with you, Quinn?" Killian asked. Connor said nothing, but even his face was drawn with concern.

"I just needed a few days off, I told you." Quinn looked at the door, but Meredith was blocking it. "I'm here now, and I'll get to work. But you all better leave me alone, or I'm outta here."

"You made my husband lie to me," Meredith accused. "You called him while in the middle of an uncontrollable shift and made him take you away."

"No, I made him not tell you, not lie about it," Quinn corrected. "Besides, I couldn't turn into a goddamn wolf in the middle of Manhattan!"

"But why couldn't you get control of Wolf?" Meredith asked. "What happened?"

"Nothing!" he roared. "Nothing at all."

"Quinn, calm the fuck down," Meredith warned.

But Wolf was growling and snarling, and he could feel the animal just ready to fight and claw out of him. Anger, pain, sadness ... the emotions were too much. He wanted Selena and, at the same time, hated her and never wanted to see her again. It was tearing him apart.

"Quinn! No!" Meredith cried as Wolf ripped out of him.

It was so fast the only thing he remembered was the sound of his clothes ripping to shreds. Wolf bared his teeth at Meredith. It wanted to destroy everything in sight.

"Fuck!" Meredith cursed as she looked at Connor. Wolf's presence was agitating Connor, and his brother was hunched over, grunting as he sought to take control of his body. Wolf was gnashing its teeth, ready for a fight.

"No!" Killian yelled. "Shift back, Quinn."

"Goddammit!" Meredith looked at Wolf. "You're buying me a new shirt, asshole!" She let out a growl, and her wolf burst out from her body in a flurry of white fur and claws. The albino she-wolf stood in front of Wolf, slowly advancing toward its brother.

Wolf snapped its teeth at the she-wolf, but the moment it sniffed the pup inside her, it backed down and laid on its back. Wolf's protective instincts had won over his need to inflict pain. The she-wolf turned to Connor and sniffed and licked his hand, until his breathing evened and he fell to his knees, letting out a pained grunt.

Quinn slowly gained control of Wolf, his limbs and snout shortening and the fur receding into his skin. He was on his hands and knees, and sweat dripped from his brow. Slowly, he steadied himself and got to his feet. The sound of the door opening, followed by a loud gasp made him snap his head up.

Evie stood by the door, her eyes wide and her mouth opened. "What happened? Oh my God, why are you naked?"

Meredith had changed back into her human form, and Connor was already taking his shirt off to hand to his sister. "God, I can't believe I saw your dick twice today, Quinn," she said. Evie blushed and covered her eyes with her hand.

Quinn caught the extra pair of jeans and shirt Killian had retrieved from his office. They were Lycans, after all, and were prepared for this kind of thing.

"What are you doing here, Evie?" Killian asked. "You said you weren't coming in today."

"I left my phone charger." She walked to her desk and retrieved the device. "Is everything okay? What happened?"

"Why don't you ask your best friend?" Quinn bit out.

Evie's face turned from concerned to distaste. "You don't know what you're talking about, so just shut up, Quinn."

"Oh yeah?" His own anger was boiling now. "She's the one who was engaged this entire time and didn't tell me."

Meredith let out a gasp. "What? Selena's getting married?"

"Yeah, surprised me too," Quinn spat. "The little liar strung me along while she was getting ready to marry her childhood sweetheart. And people say I'm the heartless one."

"Shut up!" Evie's face scrunched in anger and blood rushed to her cheeks. "Stop talking about her like that. You didn't give her a chance to explain."

"Explain what?" he asked bitterly. "That all she wanted was a good fuck from me?"

Evie leaped at Quinn, her hands extended, ready to claw his eyes out. Before she could reach him, Connor jumped between them and hooked his arms around her waist, dragging her away. "Selena told me everything!" Evie cried. "She wasn't engaged yet, but she didn't have a choice. It was marry Jason or be banished from her coven. You think she wants to be in a loveless marriage? No. But without any power, it was her only chance to gain their respect. Her entire life, her family treated her like shit while the coven did nothing." She wrenched herself away from Connor and stood in front of Quinn, eyes blazing. "No one cared for her or treated her with respect. And no one loved her, not since her mom died." She paused. "She was going to turn him down. She already bought tickets to go home and tell Jason and then her father. Selena was going to leave everything behind so she could be with you. She was in love with you, Quinn. You." Her eyes shone brightly with unshed tears. "And you hurt her and pushed her right back into their open arms," Evie said bitterly.

Quinn stood still, the pressure behind his eyes growing. Evie's words cut him like a knife, causing a fresh pain to sear through him. This time, the pain was because he hurt Selena on purpose and drove her away. It was too late now. Wolf was ripping at his insides, snarling at him for letting her go. "Fuck." He slammed his fist against the nearest wall, leaving a mark in the plaster. "I want her back." He put his hands on Evie's shoulders. "Tell me how I can get her back."

"Oh. My. God." Meredith's eyes bugged out. "You're in love with her."

"Of course I'm in love with her!" Quinn shot back.

Meredith's face turned from shock to mirth, and she started laughing. They were full-belly laughs that had her doubling over, clutching her stomach as tears streamed down her cheeks. She kept going for a full thirty seconds, then slowly began to gain her composure.

"Are you done?" Quinn asked.

"No." And she started to laugh again, clutching Killian's arm to keep herself upright. His brother bit his lip, his eyes were amused.

"All right, already, stop." Quinn rolled his eyes. "For God's sake, shut up and tell me how I'm going to get her back."

"Well, for starters," Meredith began, wiping the tears from her eyes. "You gotta stop that engagement."

"I know that. But how will I make her forgive me?"

"Oh, Quinn," she said, patting his shoulder. "You can't make her forgive you. You can only ask."

He swallowed a lump in his throat. "Shit. I said some things to her ... I don't know if she'll want to forgive me. I don't even know if she loves me."

There was a glint in Meredith's eyes. "Of course she loves you. You're her True Mate."

"What?" Quinn exclaimed. "How can you know that?"

"Well, I can't be one hundred percent certain," Meredith began. "But does she have a scent that drives you wild?"

Quinn thought of Selena's sweet butterscotch scent. "Yeah ..."

"And that didn't give you a clue? She's not a Lycan, but she has a scent?"

"Well, that did seem strange."

"And does Wolf get anxious when she's in danger or angry at you when you've pissed her off?"

"Huh." He always thought it was strange, but chalked it up to Wolf being an asshole.

"Yeah and ..." Meredith's brows knitted together. "You've finally slept with her, right? She could be pregnant with your pup right now!"

"No." He shook his head. "She's not pregnant."

"How do you know?"

"We used condoms," Quinn exclaimed. "You know, like normal, responsible people."

"Ugh," Meredith said in an exasperated voice. "Well, if you want to be really sure, then you need to inject her with your baby batter. Like, soon."

"Meredith!" Killian warned.

"What? Do you guys think I'm twelve or something?" She pointed to her belly. "Did you forget how I got this?"

"No, because you keep reminding us," Connor interjected.

"But how can you possibly know she's my True Mate? I never told you any of this until now."

Meredith bit her lip. "Er, Daric told me. He saw it in a vision."

"Right." Because aside from being able to travel across the globe in a second, Daric could also see the past and future when he touched people. If Daric saw it then ... it must be true.

"Uh, guys?" Evie interrupted. "Tonight's the engagement party where they're going to announce it to their entire coven. Glenwood Country Club. In Philadelphia."

He looked at the clock. "Shit." Philadelphia was at least a three-hour drive away. "Meredith, is Daric around?"

His sister shook her head. "Sorry, the Alpha asked him for a favor. He's out of contact for at least the next 12 hours."

"Damn." He was hoping Daric could pop him over to Philadelphia. If he drove, he just might make it. But his Range Rover was back at his house. "Did you drive today?" he asked Killian.

"No," he replied, shaking his head. "But Connor's truck is stored here in the parking garage."

All eyes turned to Connor. He crossed his arms over his chest. "No fucking way." Connor pretty much hated everything, but if there was one thing he did love, it was his black Dodge Ram. He brought it to New York even though he wouldn't be able to drive it as often as he did back in Portland. He didn't even trust a company to ship it here; instead, he put it on a rig himself and drove it across the country.

"You have to let Quinn borrow your truck," Meredith said. "Selena is ours. She's one of us now. And we can't lose her to some stupid warlock."

"We?" Connor growled. "I ain't her mate."

"Please, Connor?" Evie pleaded, grabbing his bicep with her hands. "Quinn can't let Selena marry someone else. I'll never see her again if she moves away. I want my best friend back."

Connor let out a grunt and then shoved his hands into his pocket. "Here." He tossed a set of keys to Quinn, which he easily caught. "Take care of Jolene."

"You named your car Jolene?" Evie asked.

"It's a long story," Meredith giggled.

"Thanks, bro!" Quinn said with a bright smile. "I'll take good care of her."

"You better. I just had her interior reupholstered."

"Good luck!" Meredith called as Quinn raced out the door.

23

"For crying out loud, aren't you done yet?" Jane Merlin's impatient voice shook Selena out of her trance.

"I'm almost done," she called through the bedroom door. Taking a deep breath, Selena checked her reflection in the vanity mirror one last time. It took hours, but she was able to tame her hair into a chic up-do. She also put on some makeup to cover the smudges under her eyes, but, other than that, she kept it minimal. The dress she put on was a long black evening gown she had in the closet, which seemed appropriate given the circumstances. She didn't feel like it was a happy occasion; instead, it felt like a slow march toward the end.

Selena bit her lip to keep from crying. She thought she'd exhausted all her tears, but each time she thought of Quinn ... No. It was her fault for keeping Jason a secret. She could have told him at any time, but she didn't. And now that she made her bed, she had to lie in it. With one last deep breath, she stood up and opened the door to leave her childhood bedroom.

"My, my, don't you clean up nice," Alexis sneered. She was standing outside her door, leaning against the wall. As usual, she was all dolled up, her hair and makeup perfect and her short blue dress showing off her tanned and toned legs

Selena did not have the patience to deal with her tonight. "I'm getting engaged, did you hear?"

Alexis' eyes turned into slits. "Yes, imagine that. A warlock actually wants you. Selena the Dud."

The nickname used to hurt, but now she just felt ... nothing. It was like a rocket that was shooting straight for her but suddenly fizzled out. "What, are you jealous? That Jason Ward wants me and not you?"

Alexis laughed. "You think he wants you? He's just using you to produce an heir. After all, he has everything—he's a gifted warlock, rich, handsome, has a good pedigree—the only thing left that would make his daddy and mommy happy is to have a grandchild who was descended from both Charlotte Fontaine and Magnus Merlin." She gave a snort. "Not that you turned out to have any talent." She leaned down, her face inches from Selena's and her eyes full of hate. "When you spawn another dud, Jason will realize he should have married me."

"You've been in love with him? This whole time?"

"Love?" Alexis spat. "You're such a fool, Selena. Love isn't real. You think my mother married your father for love? No. Your daddy's a rich businessman and a powerful warlock. Too bad he made her sign an iron-clad prenup that guaranteed everything would go to you if they divorced."

Her breath caught in her throat. She had no idea.

"And do you think your Lycan boyfriend loved you? Tell me, where is he now? Did he not like knowing you were engaged while you were fucking him?"

"It was you," Selena accused. "You told him about Jason."

She laughed. "Of course it was me. You thought you could hide it from me? I could see the way he looked at you that night at Merlin's. I couldn't believe he would want to sleep with a plain little thing like you and not me." She tossed her blond locks over her shoulder. "Well, when I told Leonard, he was madder than a box of cats. He told us he was going to accept Jason's proposal on your behalf and instructed us to do whatever it took to get that Lycan away from you and get you back here. So, I told him you were already engaged."

Selena felt the bottom of her stomach drop, and her vision blurred. God, her father really was willing to sink to the lowest depths to get what he wanted, even hurt his own flesh and blood. She tried to say something, but she just stood there, stunned.

"Selena!" Leonard Merlin's voice rang out loud from downstairs. "We're going to be late, come down here now."

"Congratulations," Alexis said in a sweet voice before she turned around and left her standing there.

Alexis' words washed over her. Was love really a lie? It was starting to feel like that. She thought her father loved her, but he'd been ignoring the way her stepmother and stepsisters treated her for years. And now he was forcing her to marry a man she hardly knew. She thought Jane loved her father, and she took some solace in that, but she'd been after his money all along. A small part of her had even thought Quinn loved her, but his cruel words and refusal to listen to her told her that wasn't true either.

The cold, empty feeling crept over her slowly. This would be her life now. It was this or banishment. She thought she could have survived being away from her coven if she had Quinn. But, in wanting to have it all, she lost him—the only thing that mattered.

*S*elena wasn't even sure how she got to the country club. She somehow made it from the house to Leonard's car and into the club. The function room of the Glenwood Country Club was all decked out tonight for the happy occasion. Fairy lights strung with fresh white jasmine flowers were hung overhead. The round tables scattered all over the room were covered with white tablecloths and elegant flower arrangements. Their entire coven was here to celebrate the engagement. People would stop her and offer their congratulations, and Selena nodded and smiled at them, even as she felt numb inside. Across the room, she spied Jason Ward and his parents. He was wearing a dark suit, and, even from afar, she could make out his handsome features and tall frame. When their gazes locked and he gave her a slight smile, she felt absolutely nothing.

"Hello, my dear."

Selena turned to the familiar voice. "Uncle Lucien," she said, her voice choking with emotion. "You came."

"Of course," Lucien answered, his lips forming into a sad smile. "I couldn't let you throw yourself to the wolves without any support."

She held back the tears. "Thank you," she said as she stepped into his embrace.

"Are you sure about this?" Lucien asked. "What about Quinn?"

She stiffened in his arms. "He doesn't want me, Uncle Lucien. He never did."

"I can't believe that," he said as he pulled away from her and looked into her eyes. His dark gaze captured hers. "Besides, why are you committing yourself to this sham of a marriage in the first place?" She couldn't answer him, so he let out a resigned sigh. "Remember what I told you about when you decide to stand up for yourself."

Selena almost wanted to laugh. Looking around her, with the entire coven here to celebrate the engagement, it was too late. She spied Jason again, looking handsome and regal in his suit, and she wondered if it would really be so bad. He was good looking and wealthy, and she could learn to care for him. Plus, there was the bonus of children who could grow up with magical talent.

"Selena," Leonard called as he appeared behind her. "Oh Lucien, I didn't see you there. When did you come in?"

"A few minutes ago," the other warlock answered. "I was just giving Selena my congratulations."

"Thank you, Uncle Lucien," she said weakly. "I'll see you later."

Merlin nodded at her as she allowed Leonard to drag her to their table.

"The program's about to begin," Leonard said impatiently. "We're already late. You won't even have time to have a few minutes alone with the Wards. They were looking forward to seeing you."

"Well, thank God for that." Selena shut her mouth when she realized she had said that out loud.

"You will behave, Selena," Leonard said as they sat down at their table. "You will sit there and look happy and smile at Jason Ward. Ah," he looked to the stage where a man in a tux was standing with a microphone, "You'll have to say hello to them when the host asks you to come up on stage then."

The fairy lights dimmed, and everyone hurried to their seats. Selena sat still, waiting for the program to begin.

"Good evening everyone and welcome to—who the fuck are you?" The stunned emcee looked up at the large man dressed in ripped jeans and a black shirt who marched up the steps to the stage and grabbed the microphone from his hand.

Selena's heart stopped in her chest. "Quinn?"

*I*t seemed like a good idea at the time, bursting into a room full of witches and warlocks. In fact, Wolf thought it was a *fucking brilliant* idea. Quinn had even rehearsed his entire speech on the way over. He was going to march up to Selena and declare that he loved her and they belonged together. Now he was suddenly having performance anxiety. In his ripped jeans, plain shirt, unkempt hair, and unshaven jaw, he felt even more uncomfortable in the room full of witches and warlocks dressed to the nines in formal attire. He thought it was going to be a dinner party or something small, not a decked-out ballroom with two hundred witches and warlocks, who were all currently staring at him.

"Young man," the emcee said, regaining his composure. "This is a private function. Please leave."

"Yeah? Well, I object. I object to this marriage," he declared.

"That's for the ceremony, you moron!" someone called out.

Quinn swallowed visibly. "Wow ... I thought this was going to be a small party." A loud groan from the foot of the stage caught his attention. Looking down, he saw Selena sitting at the front most table, her eyes wide with surprise. Next to her was an older warlock, probably her father. He did not look amused.

"Anyway," he continued. "Selena, you can't marry this douche bag."

"Shut up, you're the douche bag!" the same voice shouted.

Quinn ignored the voice again. "I mean, fine, I don't know if he's a douche bag, but you still can't marry him. Selena, you're my True Mate." There were several gasps from the audience and the words Lycan and wolf were whispered a few times among the crowd. "I mean, I'm not sure yet because we've been banging with condoms and she's not knocked up. But I plan to get her pregnant, as soon as she lets me put my Daddy sauce in her."

He flashed Selena a smile, but her face was hidden as she banged her head on the table and let out another groan.

"Get off the stage, moron!"

Quinn felt his blood pressure rise. "Who the fuck keeps hassling me?"

"No one wants to hear you, asshole!"

"Oh yeah? I'm the asshole? I don't come to *your* declaration of love and heckle *you*, do I?" Another audible gasp caught his attention. This time, it came from Selena. "It's true. I love you, Selena, and I can't live without you."

Selena shot to her feet. "Quinn!" she called in a desperate voice. "Get me out of here."

"You ungrateful child!" The older man beside her stood up and grabbed her by the elbow. "You will sit down and shut up, while I get security to take out this dog."

When Selena struggled to get free of her father, the older man raised his hand. Quinn instantly saw red, and Wolf was ready to tear the warlock apart. He leaped down from the stage and ran to Selena, but he was too late.

"You will let go of her and put your hand down," Lucien Merlin said in a deadly voice. He stood between Selena and her father, calm as a millpond with a glass of wine in one hand. "Or do you want her mate to rip you to shreds?"

Leonard's face went red, and his hand dropped to his side. "Selena, if you do this, you know what's going to happen."

Selena pulled away from her father. "I do. And I'm fucking glad to be out of here!" She turned to Quinn. "Let's go."

Quinn wasted no time in grabbing her hand and dragging her away, ignoring the shocked stares and indignant shouts as they rushed through the richly-decorated function room. He gave one last backward glance to make sure no one was following them, and he saw Lucien Merlin wink at him as he took a sip of his wine. They ran to the main lobby and out the door to the parking lot.

"Where's your Range Rover?" Selena asked, glancing around.

"I didn't have time to get it," Quinn explained as he led her to the other end of the parking lot. "I had to bring Jolene."

"What's a Jolene?"

Quinn nodded to the vehicle in the middle of the row of luxury cars. The jacked-up black Dodge Ram looked incredibly out of place next to all the Mercedes Benzes, BMWs, Jaguars, and Porsches. A loud beep indicated that the truck was unlocked, and Quinn helped her up into the passenger seat before swinging around and getting into the driver's side. He turned the key in the ignition, revved the engine, and tore out of the Glenwood Country Club, nearly knocking down the stunned valet who was taking a smoke break near the open exit gates.

Quinn drove away from the country club. He had been worried someone from Selena's coven might chase after them, but it was just them on the lonely country road. It would be at least another ten miles until the ramp to the highway. He breathed a sigh.

"Quinn," Selena finally said. "I can't believe you said that in front of everyone."

He flashed her a grin. "What, that we've been having responsible, protected sex or that I was going to knock you up? Cuz the first one is true and the second one will be soon."

She blushed. "No, you moron! That I'm your True Mate! Are you sure?"

"Yeah, I think so. I mean, we can't be one hundred percent

sure." Quinn saw a small clearing up ahead on the side of the road. He slowed down and maneuvered the truck into the small patch of mud. The branches and shrubs that scratched the side of the truck made him wince, but he'd figure out what to tell Connor later. "But we can try and find out."

Selena let out an indignant cry when he reached over to scoop her up out of the passenger seat and onto his lap. God, he was already hard, just being near her. If this wasn't a sign they were True Mates, then he probably had some sort of mental disorder that made him get an erection whenever he was around Selena.

"Quinn," she whispered, twisting around so she was straddling his lap. "I'm sorry. I'm so sorry for not telling you about Jason. My father—"

"Shhh ... kitten." He put a finger on her lips. "No need to apologize. Evie told me. I'm the one who should say sorry for what I said to you in the library. For not letting you explain." His chest tightened as he felt the shame of his own words. "Forgive me?"

"How about we forgive each other?" she said.

He nodded. "Agreed."

Selena leaned down and planted her lips on his. The tightness in his chest disappeared, replaced by a satisfied growl. Wolf urged him to take her now, and plant his seed in her. And he wanted nothing more than to make love to her without any barriers and then watch her belly grow with their pup in the next couple of months.

"Selena ..." He tugged at her dress, raising it over her thighs and up to her waist. Shit, he wanted to feel her naked breasts and suck on her nipples, too, but there was no time to take off the dress.

She moaned when his fingers found her panties, the front already damp. Fingers stroked her clit and her damp lips, teasing her until she was slick, then slipped into her. She rocked her hips against his fingers, grabbing on his shoulders for support. Selena let out a sharp cry as her body convulsed in a small orgasm and he continued to fuck her with his fingers. She slumped down, her face burying into the crook of his neck. Her scent teased his senses, making his cock strain painfully against his jeans. He needed her now.

"Sorry, kitten," he apologized before ripping the scrap of lace off. Selena responded by fumbling with his jeans and releasing his already hard cock. She pointed the tip at her entrance.

"Are we really going to try this here?"

"Hell, yeah," Quinn said as he grabbed her by the shoulders and sank her down on his cock. "Fuck." She was tight and wet, her inner muscles enveloping him like a snug glove. "Kitten, you feel so good." Nothing between them this time. He could feel every inch of her.

"Quinn ... I ..." Her head rolled back when he began to thrust into her. Just small movements of his hips, but she whimpered in pleasure. Selena grabbed his shoulders and began to move, grinding her pelvis down on him as her pussy squeezed him.

"Fuck ... baby ..." She felt so good. Around him and in his arms. His fingers dug into her hair, releasing it from her up do, making her wild red hair flow down her shoulders and back. Her pink lips parted as small pants escaped her mouth. She moaned his name over and over again.

"I love you, Selena," he panted. His hands gripped her hips, urging her faster and faster. "Only you. Forever."

"I can't ... I ..."

"Then don't. Just let go. I'll be here to catch you."

She let out a cry as her body shuddered and she squeezed tight around him. He couldn't control it any longer, and he came, spurting his cum inside her. His own body spasmed and the white hot pleasure sliced through him, nearly blinding his vision.

She collapsed on top of him, and he thought she said something, but his ears were still ringing. "Say that again?" he gasped.

Selena giggled. "I said, I love you too, Quinn."

He let out a sigh of relief, then grabbed the back of her head and pulled her down for a kiss. "I was beginning to think you weren't going to say it."

She smirked. "You're always so impatient."

He let out a groan as she shifted her hips. "Hmmm ... don't move, kitten."

"Aren't you uncomfortable? I can get—"

"Oh no, you're not going anywhere." He tightened his arms around her. "I'm going to make sure this works. Meredith told me all it takes is one time, the first time, but I'm not taking any chances. My buttermilk isn't going anywhere."

"What?" She looked down. "Oh. Right."

"Shit, kitten." Fuck, he didn't even ask her if she wanted a kid. "Are you ... are you regretting this?"

"Huh? No! Of course not." She laid her head on his chest. "I just never thought ..."

"Me neither." He kissed the top of her head. "I love you, Selena. And I want to have a dozen babies with you. At least."

She giggled. "Well, give me a minute here ... we don't even have one."

"Yet," he said. "Don't twins run in the family?"

24

Selena rolled over in the bed, seeking Quinn's warmth. When all she felt was the cool sheets, she opened her eyes. It was Sunday morning, and neither of them had work, so where was he? The apartment was quiet, but she did hear the distinct sound of the tea kettle's whistle, and she smiled. Quinn was making breakfast.

They arrived back in New York two nights ago and hadn't left the loft since. They hadn't even seen anyone else, either. He still hadn't figured out who was trying to hurt him, so he wanted her close. But that wasn't the only reason they spent the weekend locked up at his loft, of course. Quinn loved her, and she loved him. And they were apparently True Mates.

She wrinkled her nose and lay on her back. She had heard of the concept. After all, Quinn's sister and brother had True Mates of their own, though she wasn't sure exactly how it worked. There was something about not getting hurt and getting pregnant the first time True Mates had sex. A hand went to her belly. Could she be pregnant right now? How would she know? What if she wasn't? What if she and Quinn weren't True

Mates? Would he be disappointed? She groaned. It was too early for questions.

"Breakfast is served," Quinn announced as he walked up to the bedroom. "Selena?"

"Hmmm?" She rolled over. He was completely naked and carried a tray of food. She gave him a weak smile.

Quinn frowned and then put the tray aside. "Selena, what's wrong?"

"Nothing," she said quietly. "I'm fine."

"I made love to you three times last night and gave you at least five orgasms," he pointed out. "You should have a smile as wide as the Brooklyn Bridge." He crawled into bed and opened his arms. "Come here and tell me what's bothering you."

She scooted into his arms and put her head on his chest. His scent soothed her, but her fears remained. "Quinn ... what if ... what if I'm not pregnant? And I'm not your True Mate?"

"Kitten," he drawled, kissing the top of her head. "You are. I'm sure of it." He slid a large hand down to her belly. "In nine months, we're going to be holding a cute little bundle of joy who's going to take over our lives with his or her pooping, eating, and sleeping. And we are going to enjoy every minute of it."

She sat up and looked at him straight in the eyes. "But what if I'm not? How can you be so sure? We won't know until I'm actually pregnant, right?"

He sighed and took her hands, kissing each on the knuckles. "Selena, you are my mate. I know it, Wolf knows it." A soft rumble emanated from his chest. "And if you are not, I don't give a fuck. You're mine, and I love you. I'm gonna keep trying to knock you up because a) it's fun and b) I want to, but if it turns out we can't have a baby, then we can adopt. There are lots of kids out there who need a good home and a good mom, which you'll be."

"Oh, Quinn …" Tears streamed down her cheeks, and she squeezed him tight. "I love you so much."

"I love you too, kitten. Now," he gently pushed her back on the bed. "Eat some breakfast, and then we're going to go out and grab a pregnancy test. I don't know much about this True Mates business either, but we'll find out today. And if not, we'll go see the Lycan doctor first thing tomorrow." He got up and took the tray he had set aside. The scent of pancakes, bacon, and toast drifted into her nostrils, and Selena grabbed the fork as soon as the tray hit the bed.

"Slow down, kitten," he laughed. "There's plenty more."

They ate the food, feeding each other (though it was mostly him feeding her) until the plates were empty. Selena put the tray aside, and Quinn got up from the bed. "Let's go shower and then go to the pharmacy."

"You're so romantic," she said wryly, and let out a shriek as Quinn picked her up and walked them to the bathroom.

After a (relatively) quick shower, they dressed and got ready to leave the loft. Selena was still feeling a little nervous, but Quinn's words had made her feel better about the whole thing. And she felt the same way. True Mate or not, she loved Quinn.

"Ready?" he asked as he put his shoes on.

"Yes." Now or never.

He gave her a quick peck on the lips and grabbed the door knob. As they stepped out, Quinn suddenly froze.

"What's—" She gasped as she saw the metal barrel of the gun pointing straight at Quinn's face.

25

The smell of mildew and dirt assaulted his nose, and Quinn felt the hairs on the back of his neck stand on end. Wolf's hackles rose, and it let out a soft snarl as it sensed the other Lycan's presence.

"Don't move, don't make a sound," the Lycan said. "Step back."

Quinn wanted to fight, but looking over at Selena, he knew it was best to cooperate with this bastard. "All right buddy, don't get an itchy trigger finger." He tried to grab Selena's hand to put her behind him, but the other Lycan shook his head and shoved the barrel of the gun at his nose. "No. Leave her alone." He swung the gun at Selena, and Quinn's alarm bells went off. If Selena got even a so much as a scratch, he was going to tear this asshole apart.

"Walk over there and sit down on your hands on the couch," the Lycan instructed.

"Go ahead, kitten," Quinn said. "Do what he says."

Selena's face was ashen, but she followed him, backing up to the couch without turning around. *Good girl.* You never give your back to a Lycan. "Who the fuck are you and what do you want?"

"I'll let the boss tell you," he said with a wicked grin, turning his gun back to Quinn. "In fact, she's here."

She?

The Lycan kept his gun trained on Quinn but walked aside. A figure stepped up from behind him.

"You."

"Yes, me," Carla Martin said, her red-painted lips curling into a sardonic smile. She walked in regally in her pink Chanel suit and perfectly coiffed hair. "Oh Quinn, why couldn't you have died those other two times? Now we're going to leave a mess."

"Those weren't accidents," Selena said from where she sat.

Carla turned to her. "She's a smart one, your girlfriend. Too bad she's going to have to die along with you."

"You bitch!" Quinn shouted. "Let her go. I'm the one you want."

She tsked. "Uh uh, Quinn. Do you think I'm stupid? Yes, I want you dead, but you were too stubborn to die. Now your lovely girlfriend will have to die along with you. We can't leave any witnesses, now, can we?" She turned to her accomplice. "What do you think, Paul? Murder-suicide? Fire? Maybe we'll toss their bodies off the roof."

"Why?" Quinn asked. "Wasn't it enough that my father didn't want me? The two of you want me totally gone?"

Carla laughed. "You stupid boy. Your father doesn't even know you exist. I made sure of that," she sneered. "I'm not blind! I saw what was going on between Jacob and that whore, Anna. But I was willing to let it go, as long as they were discreet. It's hard to find good help, after all. But when she became pregnant, right when he was about to be elected to Congress, well, I couldn't let that little slut ruin his chances! So, I paid her off, told her to go away. I reasoned with her that Jacob couldn't risk having the knowledge of a love child leak out to the press. It would ruin him! I suppose the money didn't last long. I was surprised she didn't come sniffing back for more, though she was always a proud one, that Anna." Hate filled her eyes and made her face scrunch up. "I was prepared to deal with her, but not with you."

"I told you I wasn't interested in getting to know him," Quinn said. "Look, we can work this out. I promise, I won't breathe a word to anyone, just leave us alone."

"I would have, except I did a little digging to find out who you are." Carla stepped forward, her heels clicking on the hardwood floor. "You should have stayed in Portland. You're too close to us here in New York. Too close to the Alpha."

"Which is why you should just leave us alone," Quinn said. "We won't say anything."

"Not good enough." She retrieved something from her purse. A small vial. "Belladonna. Benign to humans, but lethal to Lycans. You'll drink this or Paul here," she motioned to her companion, who then trained his gun on Selena, "will shoot her."

"You'll kill her anyway," Quinn spat.

"But at least you won't have to watch," she said. "See? I can be merciful."

"No!" Selena cried. "Don't kill him!"

"Why do you want us dead?" Quinn asked.

"Because I hate you. You and your whore mother. I'm glad she's dead! I thought she was just some plaything, a little distraction, and I let Jacob have her. But, when she became pregnant with you after a few months, after we'd tried for years, well I couldn't have that!" Carla's eyes were wild now, and Quinn could sense the broken she-wolf inside her. Probably years of emotional torture and then watching another Lycan bear her husband's pup had pushed her over the edge. "I didn't have the pleasure of seeing your mother die, though I'd thought about it. Now, I'm going to watch you take your last breath."

"No!" Selena jumped up from the couch and ran towards Carla.

"Selena!" Quinn cried as Wolf instantly burst from his skin, landing on all fours in front of Carla. A gunshot rang out, and the smell of blood tinged the air. Wolf let out a howl and leaped toward Paul, who still had his arm stretched out, the gun from his hand smelling of powder and ash. They fell in a flurry of limbs and fur. The other Lycan was already starting to shift, but Wolf's massive teeth sank into his neck, blood spurting everywhere and slowing him down.

Wolf turned his head, spying Selena's prone figure on the floor and blood flowing from her shoulder. The animal let out a snarl and turned its attention to Carla.

"No," she pleaded, backing away.

Wolf let out a loud growl, trying to assert its dominance over her. Not that it needed to. Carla's she-wolf was cowering in fear, unable to shift or protect her.

"P-p-p-lease!"

But her cries fell on deaf ears. Wolf stalked her to a corner, licking its lips, anticipating the kill. She would pay for killing his mate.

"Quinn ...W-w- olf ... no ..."

Selena? Wolf's ears perked up and turned its massive head. There she was. Mate. Walking toward them. Her shoulder was all bloody, but she wasn't wincing in pain.

Selena stopped and dropped her hand to his head, running her fingers through the soft fur. "It's all right, Wolf. I'm fine." She placed her hand over her belly. "We both are."

Wolf let out a whine and rubbed its nose on her stomach. With a soft cry, it gave their body back to Quinn. As he recovered from the change and lay on the floor, Quinn reached out, seeking confirmation that Selena was okay.

"I'm fine, Quinn," she cooed, grabbing his hand and giving it a firm grip.

He got to his knees and then wrapped his arms around Selena's waist. "You're alive," he whispered over and over again. "I thought ..."

"Me, too." She ran her fingers through his hair. "The bullet got me in the shoulder, but it went through and the wound closed up. Quinn, I really am your True Mate. And I'm having your baby."

Quinn held her tighter and kissed her belly. "I love you. I thought I'd lost you."

Selena helped him get to his feet. "I'm here, Quinn. I'm here."

He breathed a sigh of relief, then stood up and wrapped her in his arms. He looked over at Paul, who was lying very still. Carla, on the other hand, had sunk to the floor, her hair disheveled and legs tucked under her, still cowering in fear.

"Let's call Killian and the others," Quinn said. "We have trash to take care of."

*S*elena assured Quinn for the hundredth time that she was okay. The wound had completely healed, and it was like she had never been harmed at all. It hurt like hell, that was for sure. She totally would not recommend being shot.

After Killian, the next call they made was to Meredith, who, along with her warlock husband, magically appeared in their living room. Without a word, they sprang into action. Meredith hauled Carla to her feet and tied her hands behind her, then tossed her on the couch. Daric, on the other hand, whisked Paul to the Medical Wing of the Lycan headquarters. While he would certainly pay for his crimes, they couldn't leave him to suffer or die.

"I knew it!' Meredith exclaimed when she saw Selena's bloody shirt. "He did it! I mean, you guys did it, right?"

Selena blushed and nodded.

"And now I'm gonna get another niece or nephew! Woohoo!" She pulled Selena into a fierce hug. Selena was glad she was indestructible now because Meredith's hug would surely have crushed any normal human being to death.

"I'm so happy for you guys," Meredith said. "Look, I'm gonna go to the balcony and make a couple of calls. Nick should know about this, if he doesn't already, so he and Grant can decide what to do with that bitch." Meredith gave her another hug and walked through the balcony doors, phone in hand.

Quinn came down from the bedroom, having put on a pair of jeans and cleaned up the blood from his body. He immediately ran to Selena and held her close. She wrapped her arms around his waist and breathed in his scent.

The doorbell suddenly rang, and Quinn reluctantly pulled away. "That's probably Killian. I should go get it."

Selena watched him walk toward the door and then open it. However, instead of letting Killian in, Quinn stood there, not moving an inch. Her senses went haywire, and she knew something was wrong. She strode to him and wrapped a hand around his waist.

"Quinn? Who's at the—" Selena couldn't stop the audible gasp from leaving her lips. Standing outside the door was an older man who was a carbon copy of Quinn. He could be Quinn a few decades from now, but he was the same height and had the same nose, cheekbones, and jawline. His hair had turned silver, though, and his eyes were brown, not the brilliant blue of her mate.

Both men stood there, not saying a word. Finally, Jacob Martin cleared his throat. "I ... I followed Carla here. She'd been acting weird for a couple of weeks now. I thought she was having an affair with that young man. Then, I saw your picture in her things."

Quinn said nothing, still stunned. Selena tugged on his hand. "Quinn, why don't you let your father in?"

He moved aside and let the old man through. Jacob nodded his thanks, still unable to take his eyes off his son. "Quinn. That's your name?"

He nodded.

Jacob gave a sad smile. "That was my grandmother's maiden name—Elizabeth Quinn. She was my favorite ..." He choked, his eyes shining bright with unshed tears. "Anna must have remembered. My boy, I'm so sorry." He reached out to grab Quinn, but he flinched the moment Jacob's hands touched his shoulder. Jacob couldn't hide the disappointment on his face as his hands dropped to his sides.

"Quinn ..." Selena soothed, rubbing his arm.

Quinn's face remained stony. "Your wife is in the living room. She tried to kill me and my mate."

Jacob's gaze flew from Quinn to Selena's face. When she nodded, his face turned purple with anger. "Carla!" he called, storming to the living room.

"Jacob!" Carla got to her feet, even though her hands were tied. "Jacob, please!"

"You hid my son from me for the last thirty years?" he roared. "And then you tried to kill him?"

"I did it for you, Jacob," Carla cried. "Please, Jacob, we couldn't have that secretary of yours go blabbing to the press about her brat!"

"Anna wouldn't have done that," he countered. "And he's my son. You had no right."

Carla's face twisted in fury. "You bastard! Did you think you could have it all? Have your whore and your pup, and me at your side, and my daddy's contacts to help you win the election? You're a fool, Jacob! I did this all for you and the clan."

"You did this for yourself, Carla," Jacob spat. "You and your father wouldn't stop harping about me becoming the first Lycan congressman. You were the one who wanted it, not me."

"Oh yeah, you sonofabitch?" Carla shot back. "See what'll happen to your campaign when I divorce you and news of your tawdry affair and your bastard child comes out. You can forget about the governor's mansion!"

"Shut up, Carla," Jacob warned. "First off, *I'm* going to divorce *you*. And you will not talk to the press. I'll talk to Grant Anderson, and he'll make you keep your big mouth shut. Or he can throw you in the Lycan Siberian Prison for attempted murder on another of our kind."

Carla let out an indignant squeak and fell back on the couch. Jacob turned to Quinn. "I'm sorry, Quinn. For what happened. I didn't know, I swear." He buried his face in his hands. "If I had known about you ... Carla and I had been trying for years, and then Anna came, and I fell in love with her ... I swear, Quinn, if I had known ..."

"Congressman Martin," Selena began. "Why don't you go to the kitchen and sit for a minute? I'll be in there shortly to make you some tea."

"Thank you ..."

"Selena."

"Thank you, Selena," Jacob said, taking her hands in his and giving them a squeeze. After one last look at Quinn, he turned and walked away.

"Quinn?" Selena asked, looking up at him. "Are you all right?" His body was rigid and his jaw tense. "Please, Quinn. Talk to me."

His head turned to her, his eyes bright. "I ... all my life, Selena. I thought he didn't want me."

"He didn't know about you."

"I'm not sure if I can believe that," Quinn said.

"I think he's telling the truth," Selena said. "The shock on his face when he saw you was real. And he looked like he was ready to kill Carla."

His shoulders slumped. "I just ... I don't know ..." He shook his head.

"Quinn," she began. "He's your father. He's going to be our kid's grandfather. I think you should give him a chance. Go and talk to him."

Apprehension filled his eyes, and he let out a sigh. "All right."

"Good," Selena said. "No matter what, I love you, okay?"

"I love you too," he choked, gathering her into his arms. He took a deep breath. "I'm going to spend my entire life making sure you're happy. You know that, right?"

Tears blinded her eyes. "I absolutely do."

EPILOGUE

*T*he Prince Albert Hotel's Imperial Ballroom was bedecked with red, white, and blue streamers, while festive lights were strung across the banisters and the balconies. A live band struck up a lively tune, and the crowd was whipped up into the frenzy as the emcee made the announcement.

"And now, let's welcome to the stage, New York's newest Governor, Jacob Martin!"

The people in the ballroom went wild, cheering and shouting as the doors opened. The crowd parted, and Jacob Martin strode through the room, accompanied by his son and new daughter-in-law. Father and son were wearing matching black tuxes while the new Mrs. Martin looked positively glowing in her blue chiffon evening gown that showed off her baby bump. The trio went up to the small dais set up in the front, and Governor Martin walked up to the podium after helping Selena to her seat.

"Thank you, everyone. Thank you for coming to tonight's Inaugural ball," Jacob said, his face beaming. "Allow me first to thank a few people who I owe a great deal to and, if it were not for them, I wouldn't be here. First, my campaign team ..." Jacob continued with his rehearsed speech, showing his gratitude to everyone who helped get him elected. "Finally," he said, clearing his throat. "As you all know, we had a bit of a last-minute surprise during the campaign, namely, my son, Quinn. And while some of my staff warned me that acknowledging him might cost me the election, I told them to go to hell." The crowd laughed. "And I'm glad I did because I'm proud to be the father of such a wonderful young man who beat the odds and turned out well, no thanks to me." Jacob gave his son a smile, his eyes shining with tears. "And, well, while I didn't get to see his first steps or hear his first words, he'll have a chance to do it with his son or daughter. Speaking of which, thank you, Selena. You've been instrumental in healing the rift between us. I'm so glad my son found a lifelong partner in you, and, if I leave this world soon, I'll be happy knowing you'll be there to take care of him." Overcome with emotion, Jacob stepped away from the podium and walked to Quinn and Selena to give them both hugs.

"You're going off script, Pops," Quinn whispered. "I think your campaign manager's about to bust a vein."

"Meh, she'll live," Jacob said. "Besides, I'm already Governor. I can do whatever the hell I want."

"C'mon, Dad," Selena urged. "They're waiting for you to open the dance floor."

"All right, but save a dance for me, okay?" Jacob's brown eyes twinkled, his expression reminding her so much of Quinn's. As she found out, Jacob Martin was every bit as charming as his son.

"I will. Now go!"

Quinn pulled Selena closer to him and buried his nose in her hair. "Kitten, you look so sexy in that dress. Your tits look amazing."

"I look fat," she said glumly. "And I'm only going to get fatter."

"You do not," he protested, then placed a hand over her belly. "You're beautiful and sexy, and I want to pull you into the nearest janitor's closet and have my way with you."

"Quinn," she admonished, "we're on a stage in front of three hundred people."

"So? They can't hear me say how I wish I could bend my wife over that podium and screw her silly."

Jacob turned his head from where he was standing by the foot of the stage and gave them a wink.

"Except the Lycans," Selena said wryly. "Behave, please. And dance with your wife."

"Only because you asked nicely."

Quinn led her to the dance floor where he gave her a playful spin that set her into a fit of giggles before pulling her close into his arms. As the music played and the other couples danced around them, she laid her head on his chest, tuning out the rest of the world and listening to the beating of his heart.

The last few weeks were certainly a whirlwind. Between Carla and Paul being sent to Lycan prison, trying to repair the relationship between Quinn and Jacob, getting engaged, having a quickie wedding, watching the campaign, and, of course, gestating a magical Lycan baby, Selena was exhausted. But the worst was over now. Quinn and Jacob were slowly healing, together, and his father's public acknowledgment of their relationship was a big factor in helping with that. It was horrible at first when the news broke. They were being followed by reporters all day long, but that pretty much died down a few days later when the next big scandal hit the headlines.

"What are you thinking about?" Quinn asked.

"About families," she said.

Quinn frowned. "Are things okay with your father?"

Selena sighed. "Uncle Lucien says I'm not banished from the

coven. He won't tell me how, but I suspect he had a lot to do with that. So, I'm free to visit Philadelphia and mom anytime."

"But?"

"But ... I don't know." She shrugged. "I just ... he's my dad, you know? It still hurts ..."

"I know, kitten." He pulled her close. "Whatever you decide, whether you want to try and work things out or never talk to him again, I'll support you."

"Thank you."

"Your stepsisters on the other hand ..." He gave a distasteful grimace.

Selena giggled. "Did they try to get tickets to the ball?"

"They did, and I told them to fuck off. Then a couple hours ago, I saw them trying to sneak in here, telling security they were the Governor's son's favorite sisters-in-law."

"Ha! Hopefully, security didn't let them in."

"I circulated their pictures to the staff. They won't be getting in here."

"Good," Selena replied. Katrina and Alexis would always be part and parcel with her father, something she had to accept if she ever wanted to repair that relationship, but she vowed never to let them or anyone else walk all over her again.

"I love you," he whispered in her ear.

She looked up at him, into his clear blue eyes, and her heart fluttered, even after all these months. She once thought that loving Quinn would only lead to heartache and pain. Sure, there were days when she didn't know whether to kiss him or drown him, but it was all worth it. Loving Quinn was freedom; it was giving him the best of herself, but also getting the best of him in return. And for Selena, that would be enough for the rest of her life.

EXTENDED EPILOGUE

Five years later ...

"Licence and registration, please, sir," the stern-faced cop said as Quinn rolled down the window.

"I told you you were going too fast," Selena grumbled from the passenger seat.

"Well, if you didn't take so much time getting ready, we wouldn't be late," Quinn answered as he fished his wallet from his pocket. He took out a plastic card and handed it over to the police officer. "Here you go, sir."

The officer took the card and held it up. He frowned and pulled his sunglasses down the bridge of his nose, then gave the license a second glance. "Sir, is this a joke?"

"What? No officer, I would never joke with you."

Selena guffawed.

"Is that so, Mr. McFuckface?"

"Mister what?" Quinn grabbed the card and scanned the front.

"Mommy, daddy, the officer said a bad word!" Four-year-old Lizzie screamed from the back seat.

"Why is McDuckface a bad word?" her adopted brother, Anthony, asked. Meanwhile, the newest addition to their growing family, little Jacob, gurgled happily in his car seat.

"Oh my God, you still have that thing?" Selena asked, slapping her hand over her eyes. "I gave you that library card years ago!"

"Of course," Quinn said. "It's the first gift you ever gave me." He took out his wallet and handed the correct card to the cop. "Sorry, officer. Here's my real license."

"Hmm ..." The officer looked at the card.

"He has to put money in the swear jar!" Lizzie exclaimed. "He said a bad word!"

"Elizabeth Eowyn Martin!" Selena hissed. "Keep quiet, please."

The officer took off his sunglasses. "Well, if I don't have to put money in the swear jar, maybe I can let you off with a warning?"

Selena let out a sigh of relief. "Thank you, officer. And, no, you don't have to put money in the swear jar."

"But mommy, that's not fair! You made me put a dollar in when I called that lady on TV who was mean to Grampa a b—"

"Shush, Lizzie!" Selena let out a sigh.

The police officer was trying to suppress a laugh as he handed Quinn his license back. "All right, Mr. Martin, drive safe and have a good day." He gave the kids a final wave and walked back to his car.

As soon as Quinn pulled the window up, he breathed a sigh of relief. "Whew. Never thought I could use our adorable children to get out of a ticket."

"Yeah, well, now we're really late, so let's get a move on."

"All right then. Everyone strapped in?" He turned around, looking at his three kids and then Selena. It sounded clichéd, but the sight of them never failed to give him that warm, fuzzy feeling in his chest. He once asked Selena if she regretted not having witch or warlock children, and she replied that all their kids were magical. He certainly agreed.

He never dreamed he could be so happy, despite the mess and the chaos of having two toddlers of the same age and an infant. They adopted Anthony not long after Lizzie was born. They had been touring a public hospital with his father when they saw him. Anthony had to be put in an incubator because his mother had been an alcoholic and drug user up until she gave birth prematurely. She then died soon after. None of the staff thought he would make it, but he was a little fighter. Selena and Quinn visited him every day and fell in love with him. With their connections and because no one wanted a sickly baby, they were able to take him home and formally adopt him after a few months. Not only had Anthony survived, but he was growing up into a healthy and bright little boy.

"Finally," Quinn groaned as they approached the Anderson mansion on Long Island. It was a long weekend, and Grant and Frankie were hosting another of their famous barbecues. The food and drinks were always phenomenal and free flowing, plus, with the amazing views of the ocean, it was always a treat to come here.

"Look, it's Jolene!" Lizzie said in an excited voice as she jabbed her finger against the glass, pointing at the black Dodge Ram that was parked a few spots away. "Uncle Connor's here!"

"Yay! Uncle Connor!" Anthony echoed.

"I can't believe Connor is the 'fun uncle' now," Quinn groaned. "That was supposed to be my shtick."

Selena laughed. "Yeah, now you're just mean daddy, especially when you give them homework."

While most people would have thought Quinn would've been more the laid-back and carefree parent, he was actually the opposite. He was so worried that his kids would turn out to be juvenile delinquents (like him) that he had become a strict disciplinarian. He wanted his children to grow up smart and with a good work ethic, so he started teaching them to read and count at an early age. He couldn't wait to get them in front of a computer.

"Hmmm ..." He looked over at the jacked-up truck. "Think Connor'll sell me Jolene this year?"

"He loves that thing; he'll never sell it."

"What if I tell him why I want it?"

"Don't you dare!" Selena turned red. "You will not tell him we conceived Lizzie in his truck," she whispered. "Remember his reaction when he saw that scratch on the door?"

"Yes. But remember how fun that night was?"

She turned even redder. "Yes," she said with a small smile. "Now, let's get everyone out of the car and go get some food."

"Yeah, before all the pregnant Lycans finish everything off," Quinn moaned as he unbuckled his belt.

They unpacked the car and Selena carried Jacob in his car seat, while Quinn had one toddler in each arm. When they reached the backyard, Anthony and Lizzie squirmed out of their father's arms as soon as they saw their cousins and friends piling on top of Sebastian, playing their favorite game, Catch the Dragon. Connor was chatting with Dante by the grill, handing the chef a cold beer. His brother turned his head when he heard the familiar squeals of Lizzie and Anthony, and then waved to Quinn and Selena.

Selena and Quinn walked over to the adults who were sitting in the lounge chairs and enjoying the perfect weather. She put the carrier down and picked up Jacob, bouncing the chubby baby in her arms.

"Daric thinks we're going to have a girl," Meredith announced as Selena sat down on the empty love seat. Quinn plopped down beside her and grabbed her legs, draping them over his lap.

"Did you see it?" Selena asked the warlock.

"I have a good feeling about this one," Daric said with a cryptic smile.

"What happened to you guys, anyway?" Meredith asked. "Why are you so late?"

Selena rolled her eyes and recounted what happened, including the incident with the police officer.

"Quinn McFuckface? You really gave him that name?" Meredith chuckled.

"It seemed like a good fit at the time," Selena answered, giving her husband a wry look.

"Well, ha ha," Quinn mocked. "The joke's on you, Mrs. McFuckface."

Selena laughed out loud. "Yes, I guess it is."

THANKS FOR READING!

But before you go, do want to read (**hot, sexy and explicit**) bonus scenes from this book? Join my Reading Group now! You'll get access to my super secret goodies page on my website where you can download this bonus scenes and some free e-novels. Go to http://aliciamontgomeryauthor.com/mailing-list/ and join now.

I love hearing from readers and if you want to tell me what you think do let me know at alicia@aliciamontgomeryauthor.com

Connect with Alicia Montgomery:
http://aliciamontgomeryauthor.com/
https://www.facebook.com/aliciamontgomeryauthor/
https://twitter.com/amontromance

ABOUT THE AUTHOR

Alicia Montgomery has always dreamed of becoming a romance novel writer. She started writing down her stories in now long-forgotten diaries and notebooks, never thinking that her dream would come true. After taking the well-worn path to a stable career, she is now plunging into the world of self-publishing.

Sexy shifters, billionaires, alpha males, and of course, strong, sexy female characters are her favorite to write. Alicia is a wanderer, along with her husband, they travel the world and have lived in various spots all over the world.

AUTHOR'S NOTE

Being one myself, I know exactly what "middle child syndrome" feels like. Quinn is my middle child, not just because his book lands smack dab in the middle of Lone Wolf Defenders, but he really took a lot of my attention, and quite possibly, is the reason I'm wearing a sling right now (ouch, sprained wrist ligament).

But, just as I thought, he was a lot of fun to write. When I first started writing him back in Tempted by the Wolf, I knew he was going to be a different kind of hero - not the usual dark and brooding character, but someone more lighthearted and maybe a bit (okay, a LOT) of a smart ass. I knew he needed someone who could match him, and I do hope Selena was every bit the brave, sassy, and large-hearted heroine you thought she would be.

Now, onto Connor! If you noticed something in the extended epilogue and you're thinking what I think you're thinking- don't panic!! I promise all will be explained and he will have his own HEA. I have lots of surprises in store for that book, both inside and out!

It's always a joy to hear from readers, so please do drop me a line at alicia@aliciamontgomeryauthor.com and tell me what you think. I hope you leave me a review (hint hint) if you enjoyed reading Loving Quinn. But if you didn't and want to explain why, then I'd love to hear that too. It helps me get to know my audience and gauge their interest, and most of all, get to know who you all are in some way.

Thanks for reading!

All the best,

Alicia